No More Superhumans

Freedom or Death

By Shadow Kai Writing Group

M.R. Richardson

Shadow Kai Writing Group
Acknowledgment

I'd like to thank you, the buyer, for taking a chance on a new story. You won't be disappointed.

No More Superhumans

Table of Contents

Shadow Kai Writing Group

Chapter One

Norway was nothing like Argentina, Talon thought. Not that he had expected many similarities when he'd upped sticks and moved into a tiny hut in the mountains by Olden, but he'd guessed that an Argentinian hero such as himself might receive a warmer welcome. But no. He was freezing his balls off in a lodge smaller than his bedroom at home, and what's worse, he was sharing it with two other men.

Alvarez and Yaco were serious men, and they spent many hours seated in front of their log fire, talking tactics. Talon knew he was there on a technicality. He'd discovered his father's plot to assassinate the Queen of England by accident, and insisted that he tag along. He had nothing better to do, right?

His father, Savio, had fought in the Falklands War. Talon had always admired his dad's bravery and planned to follow in his footsteps, making his country proud. Now, he had an opportunity to humiliate Britain, the way the Argentinians had been humiliated in the seventies by their enemy.

With his father scoping out Buckingham Palace for weak points, however, he was beginning to regret his decision. In three months, he still hadn't seen an ounce of action. When would the payout be, he wondered? When would they earn revenge for everything the British had put them through under Thatcher? He had little to live for, but the fear of more blood being spilled. As the hours and days ticked by in that cold Olden hut, Talon's patience wore thinner and thinner.

That was, of course, before the helicopter flew into the mountains and dropped six superhumans from the sky.

Chapter Two

"It's raining superheroes," Little Royal sang smugly as she activated her parachute. Nickolas Ilon - better known to the world as Mr. AC - shook his head, his metal suit creaking a little as he did so. He was the only one of the six without a parachute - his power suit did the heavy lifting, literally and metaphorically. It had been a long flight from the USA to intercept this enemy, so he was glad that his body could relax in the suit, even if his mind couldn't.

"Focus, girl. You'll get yourself killed."

"Nah," Little Royal shouted, the wind carrying her voice. "Sweet Sixteen is calling my name. You shouldn't worry so much. You take all the fun out of the job."

Little Royal the youngest on the team at fifteen. Nickolas rolled his eyes. He'd never been one for worrying. He was impulsive, happy to live on a whim until the day he died. But something about the young girl made him feel protective as if she were his own daughter. He still couldn't believe that her parents - who acted as monarchs in a tribe in South Africa – had allowed Little Royal to gallivant across the world on crazy missions. Still, Nickolas was always glad to have her. Out of his entire team of young heroes, she was by far the strongest. And in a team of superheroes, he needed strong characters.

"You might be a princess, but you need to stop acting like one. This shit is dangerous. Get your head in the game."

"Thanks, *Mom*. I'll keep that in mind."

Nickolas couldn't help smiling. She'd always been far too sassy for her own good. They were close to the ground at this point, and three men had exited a tiny lodge on the mountain, prepared with machine guns.

"Oh *shit*, they mean business," Ralf Dungaree cried, grinning. Dungaree the lovable dumb muscle of the team. His parachute was struggling to hold the weight of his heavy body, so it was fortunate that they were close to the ground. His muscles strained against his sleeveless jean jacket and he flexed his muscles, ready for action.

"Language," Little Royal said with a grin. She veered her parachute to the side to avoid a set of bullets, before landing gracefully. "That all you got, boys? I've got something better."

Little Royal let the laser beams exit her hands as the others landed. She toyed with the men from the lodge, aiming the beams in the snow and leaving behind scorched earth. One of the men, the youngest, fell to the ground in a panic. Nickolas felt sorry for him. Everyone always underestimated the powers of the supers. But that was before his team showed up. After, no one doubted their powers.

"Alright power suit, do your thing," Nickolas murmured to himself. He activated the bullet setting in each of his hands, with the flick of a switch within the suit, and aimed.

"Bullets deploying in three, two, one…"

Nickolas' suit took a few bullets, but within seconds, he was unloading his own, faster than any machine gun. Like Little Royal, he avoided making any fatal hits. They needed captives to take back to the USA. That was the deal. But he saw no harm in a little collateral damage. After all, these assholes were trying to kill the Queen of England. They were the bad guys, not him. He was there to do a job, but it didn't mean he couldn't have a little fun while he did.

Little Royal was having fun too. She was going to tire herself out the way she was going, somersaulting to avoid bullet wounds, and just plain showing off. Nickolas was taking most of the damage, though nothing could penetrate his suit. Not even the bullets that were bouncing off him repeatedly.

No More Superhumans

Di-Man touched on the ground and cut away his parachute. Di-Man the playboy and youthful influencer. Within seconds, he was zipping through the snow, jumping through pockets to reach other dimensions and returning within seconds, laughing all the way. Demonica and Frost – the last two members of the team - were last on the ground, but Nickolas could already see that something was wrong. Frost being seventeen is the only other teenager on the team. Frost was clutching at his chest and Demonica supported him with one arm, her eyes red as she focused her energy on destroying the lodge and its contents.

"Man down!" Demonica cried, her voice other-worldly as she used her powers. Demonica the sassy sorceress with strange and mystic powers. Nickolas cursed loudly. He allowed his bullet to clip the leg of the eldest of the terrorists. The man fell down immediately, crying out in agony, but Nickolas had no sympathy. He was certain this was the one who'd shot down Frost.

"Damn it...let's finish this, people. Quit messing around."

"My pleasure, *boss*," Di-Man said with an edge to his tone. He jumped twice more before locking the first gunman in a headlock. One swift punch from Ralf knocked the youngest terrorist out cold, though he'd been cowering in the snow since the short battle began. Di-Man struggled to keep the final shooter in the headlock, so Ralf roughly pushed him aside, taking over. It looked like it took him no effort at all to keep the terrorist in place, despite the captive struggling with all his might. *That's Ralf for you*, Nickolas thought, *thick as pig shit, but the strongest guy ever to live.*

For the first time since landing, Nickolas moved, his power suit making heavy footprints in the snow. Each step echoed in the lonely mountains, and the two terrorists that were still conscious had the sense to finally look scared. In less than a few minutes, they'd annihilated their defenses, but at what cost?

"You scumbags are going to rot in jail," Nickolas said, pressing his heavy metal boot down on the floored gunman. The man whimpered quietly beneath his boot and Nickolas added more pressure.

"You just shot down a young boy. I could kill you right now," Nickolas hissed. In moments like this, he often lost his cool, but his team was good at bringing him back down to earth. Little Royal appeared at his side, folding her arms over her skinny body.

"Why kill him when you can watch him suffer for what he did?" Little Royal said quietly. She didn't take much seriously, but when someone hurt one of her people, God help them. She scuffed her boot, kicking snow on the man's face. He sputtered in disgust and Little Royal turned to Nickolas.

"The helicopter will be landing in five. We need to get Frost on it first, if he has any hope of making it through."

"We don't have time to wait. I'll take him. Di-Man, you're in charge."

Di-Man saluted him solemnly. "You got it, boss."

Nickolas made his way over to Demonica and Frost. He was glad his face was hidden by his mask. He saw where that damned bullet hit. There was no way Frost was pulling through a hit like that. Nickolas' face screwed up in anger and sadness.

"Suit, redirect to the helicopter. Send a signal to the medical team on board."

"You got it, Mr. AC."

Nickolas scooped Frost's limp body in his arms. At just seventeen, Frost was one of the newer heroes on the team. Still unsure of his powers. Still terrified of missions. Now, Nickolas was paying the price for encouraging him to come along. His fate had been sealed before he'd even hit the ground.

Frost lay still in his arms, but Nickolas didn't pronounce him dead. He didn't want to upset Demonica, despite the patch of red Frost had left in the snow speaking louder than any words. Nickolas took off, allowing the computer in his suit to steer. The computer was working overtime, already scanning Frost's body.

"No heartbeat detected. Loss of blood at twenty nine percent. Shot wound to the heart. Fatal."

"Yes, computer, thank you. I can see that one for myself."

No More Superhumans

Nickolas and the computer were quiet as they approached the helicopter. The medical team opened the doors for them to get inside, and they landed safely. But of course, Frost would never be alive again.

Nickolas opted to step outside of his suit once in the safety of the helicopter, sitting on a bench and allowing the noise of the aircraft to drown out his thoughts. He loved his job. He really did.

But it didn't mean there weren't dark days.

Chapter Three

Nickolas felt extremely lucky to be allowed at the funeral of Frost - known to his friends in school as Carter Enright. His mother wasn't impressed with them, blaming the boy's death entirely on Nickolas' squad.

It was a full house at the church, so Nickolas and his band of misfits took a seat at the back. Not one of them looked right. Little Royal was too lavishly dressed, and Ralf was still wearing his sleeveless denim jacket (though he'd made the effort to put a black shirt and tie on beneath it.) Di-Man was intent on looking stylish, so though he was wearing all black, the leather jacket wasn't exactly suitable. Demonica had been in a rage since the incident, so her eyes glowed red for the entire ceremony. Nickolas despaired for them all. Their squad was a mess. In a simple mission, they'd lost one of their own. Things couldn't really get much worse.

And yet they could. At the burial, Nickolas spent the entire time avoiding Mrs. Enright's gaze as she shot daggers in the direction of him and his team. Even after Carter was lowered into the ground and she left her son behind, Nickolas couldn't shake off the feeling of her eyes boring into him.

Nickolas and his gang stayed behind for over an hour to pay their respects, but the others were beginning to get restless. While Nickolas stared at the fresh mounds of dirt covering Frost's coffin, Ralf slapped a meaty hand on his shoulder, causing him to wince.

"Ah come on, boss. Let the kid go. You know that none of this was our fault."

No More Superhumans

"Is that so?" Nickolas asked quietly. "Wasn't it us that took a child on a dangerous mission? Wasn't it us that left him behind at the back of the pack? We should have had eyes on the kid."

"You had eyes on Little Royal," Di-Man pointed out as he stepped through a pocket in another dimension to join the men at the graveside. "She's more of a handful than he ever was."

"Hey," Little Royal snapped. "I know what I'm doing. The boss is right. Frost had no place on our team. He wasn't anywhere near our standard."

"Have some respect," Demonica said in her low, menacing tone. "I've told you all a million times before. We're equal in this. We all made it here because we're special." Her face softened as she looked Nickolas in the eye. "But shit happens. It's a part of the job."

Nickolas knelt at the graveside. At the top of Carter's headstone, a snowflake had been carved to commemorate his power. Nickolas traced it with his finger. "But it shouldn't happen," he said after a long pause. "We're meant to be unbeatable. Our team is in shambles. You say we're born for this life, and yet we lost a man out there."

"We also caught three terrorists," Demonica argued. "Say what you want, but that's worth something at least."

Nickolas scoffed. "Was it worth Carter's life?"

No one responded to his question. Ralf chuckled darkly to himself, trudging away from the grave in his heavy leather boots. Little Royal followed next, and so on, until only Nickolas and Demonica remained.

As much as she had been trying to stay strong, Nickolas was watching the resistance in Demonica dissipate. Holding it together was only making her emotions build up, and Nickolas was preparing for them to flood out. He watched her kneel in front of the grave, reading the sparse inscription, with tears in her eyes. She shook her head slowly.

"I know you're right. It wasn't worth it. Carter...Carter was special. And not just because of his powers. He was a good friend to me. I never knew anyone as sweet as him. I'm going to miss him a lot." Demonica looked up at Nickolas with watery eyes. "But we can't give up the fight. We do good things, Nickolas. If we don't, no one else will. We're the only ones capable of putting up enough force to defeat evil. And yes, we're a bit of a rag-tag bunch...but we will get better. You think we'll get better, right? Not every mission will be like this one...will it?"

Nickolas didn't respond. Out of all of them, he had been in the superhuman industry the longest. He was the eldest, the natural leader, the one who called the shots...and yet he wasn't much better than they were, really. He didn't know anything about saving the world. Hell, there was a time when he understood nothing about politics in his own country, let alone saving the world.

He had used his brain to create something incredible - a power suit that would save the world a million times over - but he hadn't been prepared for how he would inspire others. He'd thought he was doing it simply for his own benefit.

It used to be just him helping clean up the streets, back in the day. New York had a lot of scumbags, and he always reckoned he was good for lending a helping hand, but not much more. He caught a few robbers, put a few drug dealers behind bars, that kind of thing. He loved his job. He loved the attention it brought him from women, and how it made him feel like a hero. Essentially, he was just being a nuisance to the police, interrupting their work and taking all the glory, but he hadn't cared much. It was all about him.

And then the experiments started in labs all over the world. People started to go missing, appearing months later with strange new powers and embarrassing stage names. His work had pushed others to try and defy the laws of humanity, only on a larger scale. He could remember some of the ones that made it out of those labs - Crunch; a man who went mad, and went around crushing people's necks with nothing but his bare hands, after acquiring super strength; Flora, a young girl who was tortured in a lab until she managed to learn to sprout flowers from the ground; and Beam, a young man who went blind after discovering that his power was to create a bright light from his hands. In those days, superhumans were just dangerous experimental disasters who did more harm than good.

No More Superhumans

A lot of people died before the real heroes emerged. Demonica was one of the lucky ones, as were the rest of Nickolas' team. They made it out alive, with powers that were useful enough to land them all jobs. They were all rich and famous, and the younger ones were stars on social media. Nickolas had been rich before. He didn't need all the added extras that came with the job. In fact, if he could go back, he suspected he would never have started on this treacherous journey in the first place. It had been good for a while, but now, his boyish experiment to make him a better man had landed him with more responsibility, more stress and a dead kid that would forever be on his conscience.

And now, Demonica, barely out of childhood herself, was asking him to tell her that it was all going to be okay. What the hell was he supposed to say to that? Nothing about this was ever okay. That's why he couldn't even promise that history wouldn't repeat itself. Any of them could die at any moment. People were always forgetting the most important fact of all; they were superhuman, not invincible.

Superhuman was still human. *And what does a human do to save another's feelings?* Nickolas questioned. *They lie.*

"This will be the last time something like this happens. I promise."

Demonica seemed satisfied by the answer. For the first time in days, her eyes weren't glowing their angry shade of red. Now, her soft brown eyes had returned, and Nickolas could convince himself for a moment that Demonica was just a normal girl. Not a deadly killing machine. Just a girl who has lost her friend.

Nickolas felt his phone ring in his pocket, so he stepped away from the graveside to take the call. He saw as he picked up that it was his boss, Regina Hall, at the S.H.O. - the Superhuman Organization.

"Mr. AC," she said in way of greeting. "How was the funeral?"

Nickolas glanced over at Demonica, who was still crouched beside her friend's graveside. "As well as could be expected, I suppose."

"No fights with Carter's mother?"

"I suspect she would have had words with us if it was any other day."

"Well, at least you managed to avoid some conflict. But that's not why I called. Do you want the good news or the bad news?"

"Bad. Always."

"Damn, wasn't expecting that. Well, the bad news is that the terrorists have escaped. They paid off the prison guard and made it away without a hitch."

Nickolas' heart sank like a brick at the bottom of a lake. "So, you're saying that the kid died for nothing?" he hissed.

"Well, when you put it that way…"

Nickolas swore loudly, attracting the attention of Demonica. He stalked further away to continue the conversation.

"What the hell, Regina? That's not just bad news. That's catastrophic news."

"Well, call it what you want to. It's happened now."

"Then what's the good news? It better be bloody good."

"The good news is we've implanted them with special chips. We suspected something would go wrong, so when we brought them in sedated, we put them in the back of their necks. Each chip has a GPS signal, so we will be able to track where the terrorists go next, and whenever they become useless to us, there's also a detonation setting. With this kind of tech, we can follow them without their knowing, but eliminate the threat in seconds if needs be. They might lead us to a bigger organization, and then we can take them all down."

Nickolas rolled his eyes. "Until they pay some dumb guard even more next time and disappear again."

"Have some faith, Nick. This could be a good thing. And besides. You took them down easily. Nothing the team can't handle, right? Especially with the S.H.O. behind you."

Nickolas wasn't so sure. After the team's most recent loss, nothing was certain to him, not even their own survival. And the S.H.O. may be his work-base technically, but he didn't trust them. It was comprised of the scientists that had conceived the newest generation of superheroes, of money-hungry social influencers wanting an in on the latest trends in superhuman culture, and of exploitative women like Regina, using the mutant race as a semi-human shield for the world's many problems. Nickolas was certain he didn't want a part in it any longer, but what choice did he have anymore? This was a world of his making, and he had to live with it.

Chapter Four

Talon knew he was lucky to be alive. He wasn't certain how, if he was honest. He'd sustained injuries against the supers, then been thrown in jail, and then before he knew it, he was on the run again after Yaco and Alvarez had negotiated their freedom. He knew without them he'd be a goner, and he was grateful that they'd kept him around, even if they only did so in the knowledge that Talon's father would end them otherwise.

But the USA was not as easy to hide in as Norway. Considering they had already been caught once, Talon was surprised at how long they'd hung around in New York City. He kept asking Yaco and Alvarez why they hadn't yet smuggled themselves out of the country, but neither of them would answer his questions. They insisted that he only ever knew what he needed to. Talon thought that was probably because he'd be tortured for information if he was caught again. He really didn't like to dwell on that thought.

But he was starting to question his companions anyway. Since their escape, they were becoming increasingly more brazen, openly walking around New York's streets without a hint of a disguise. He went along with it, because his father had long since drummed it into him that everyone - literally *everyone* - knew how to act better than he did. But it made him scared. Especially as they were now in a crowded coffee shop, apparently waiting for one of their 'dear friends' to show up.

It was hard to miss the pair who entered the cafe. The first looked oddly familiar - a handsome African American man dressed entirely in leather, his outfit accessorized with a random assortment of belts, rips and functionless buttons. Behind him was a woman beautiful enough for it to be considered likely that she was the man's girlfriend - a gorgeous couple, but an odd one. She too wore an entirely leather outfit, and her white blonde hair was fashioned in an intricate twist. Talon noted that they were dressing to be noticed, and it was working. In fact, their look was reminiscent of the crazy characters that had defeated Talon and his crew only days earlier.

Were these two superhumans?

Every head turned toward the door as the pair locked hands and walked to the front of the queue. The male barista behind the counter watched them in discomfort, clearly not impressed by their antics, or their attire.

"Excuse me, you'll have to go to the back of the queue," the timid barista said. The strange pair looked at one another, cocking their heads almost simultaneously.

"What do you think, honey? Do you want to go to the back of the queue?" the man asked. She smiled sweetly, shaking her head fervently. The man turned back to the barista with a shrug.

"Sorry. No can do."

"Sir, I would appreciate-"

The man held out his hand, making a slow motion in front of the barista's face like he was turning a doorknob. The barista turned pale, his eyes rolling back into his head. Talon stood up in terror, ready to run for the door, but Alvarez grabbed his arm and forced him to sit down again.

"Don't be a fool," he hissed to the younger man. "Do you want to be on the wrong side of that man?"

Talon didn't, of course, but he was beginning to worry that they were going to draw far too much attention to themselves. If the feds weren't already after them, they would be when they discovered an evil superhuman strolling through New York. It didn't occur to him that maybe that was the idea. That maybe this kind of performance was designed to say *look, I'm here, and I'm here to stay.*

After a few moments, the barista stammered out several words.

"What...would...you...like...to drink?"

The woman in leather laughed, shaking her head. Some of the customers were running away already, but others stayed, transfixed by the scene before them. Talon wished he could be anywhere else. Not even his father's henchmen were making him feel safe anymore. But he stayed because, more than anything, he feared what his father would say if he discovered his son had run away like a coward.

"I'll take an herbal tea and a hot chocolate, if it's no trouble," the man said smoothly, his smile both entirely charming and chilling. "And we'll have table service, please."

"It's a little loud in here, too, don't you think?" the woman in leather commented, gesturing around her at the silent customers. "So many thoughts bouncing around…can you make them leave, honey? I want to clear my head…"

"Anything for you, princess," the man said with a cruel smile. The whole thing was like a comedy bit, but Talon didn't get the punchline. He very much suspected he was about to find out.

The barista returned hastily with the leather clad pair's order. The man seemed to release his hold on the barista with a flick of his wrist and the barista stumbled backward into a coffee machine. Almost immediately, the man began to motion both of his hands in a strange manner, like he was shaping pottery in midair. The lights in the room began to crackle, and then the filament in each bulb burst. The coffee machinery began to shake and groan, before ceasing to work altogether. Talon watched as energy seemed to collect in the man's gesticulating hands, a silver ball of light pulsating between his fingers. Then, he turned to the queue of people that still remained, who all watched in horror as the electricity seemed to feed into his veins. His eyes almost sparkled, and Talon was strangely captivated by the sight, despite the terror in his heart.

The light in the man's hands disappeared completely, leaving the room cold, dark and silent. The room had been completely stripped of electricity. His female companion tutted, cocking her head to the side.

"Oh dear. It looks like the store is closed," she said, pouting her lip dramatically. "Time to make everyone leave, right, honey?"

No More Superhumans

Her partner was already grinning, his hand focused toward a table. A young businessman seated with a cappuccino looked completely horrified. He seemed to catch on that he was the next victim, but he couldn't do anything about it. His legs kicked desperately as the man in leather lifted him with nothing but the power of his own mind, suspending him in midair. Then, with a casual flick of his wrist, the businessman was thrown against the glass window, shattering it with the force of his body.

It was the final straw for the remaining customers. With screams and cries of horror, they left the store. In a matter of seconds, the only people that remained were the leather couple and Talon's group. The man sighed and picked up his drinks, heading over to their table and sitting down opposite Yaco.

"Enjoy the show, Alvarez?" the man in leather said, settling on a chair and putting his clunky boots up on the table. Talon flinched as the cups on the table jumped on the impact. "Where's the boss man, hmm?"

"Coming," Alvarez growled simply. "You have made a mess. He will not be pleased."

"It's not his coffee shop, is it?"

"You are drawing too much attention," Yaco butted in, mirroring Talon's thoughts. The man shrugged as the woman in leather began to massage his burly shoulders.

"I told him that if he wants my help, it will be on my terms. And I guess I felt like making a mess today. Besides, I thought he wanted to see what I can do."

"He's not even here yet. He missed your sorry little performance."

The man in leather. "You think you boys can do better, huh?" He turned to Talon with malice in his eyes. "What about you, tough guy? You think you can take me on?"

Talon shook his head furiously. The man smirked at him and then leaned over the table with his hand outstretched for Talon to shake. After what he'd seen the man do with his hands, he wasn't sure he wanted to touch him, but if he didn't, he was certain there would be consequences.

He shook the hand quickly, certain he could still feel static lingering on the man's skin.

"Everyone calls me Tri-Man," he told Talon, who suddenly understood where he knew him from. He looked almost the spitting image of Di-Man, the superhuman he'd fought only days earlier. Tri-Man was perhaps a little older, and his powers surpassed anything that Talon had seen before. Even Demonica, that strange little witch woman, seemed weak in comparison to Tri-Man.

But why was Tri-Man hanging around with a bunch of escaped convicts? Why was he entering coffee shops and showing off his powers by terrorizing the people there? Didn't he want to use his powers for good? Clearly not, if this was anything to go by.

"This here is my lovely girlfriend...Mindeater," he said in a sinister purr. Mindeater grinned at Talon.

"It's because I can read your thoughts...every single one," Mindeater informed him. Talon gulped. Had she been able to hear all his thoughts about running away?

"Yes," she said in response. Talon blushed, hanging his head. He felt exposed.

Tri-Man, shaking his head. "You have nothing to worry about from us...as long as you do as we say. You answer to us now."

"We still answer to Savio," Alvarez cut in confidently, as though Tri-Man was an annoying child and not a terrifying entity. Alvarez glared at Tri-Man. "As do you. This is his mission, and you will honor his wishes."

Tri-Man inspected his nails with a cold smile. "For now."

It was that moment when Savio himself decided to show up. Talon watched his father enter the shop with an air of importance and grace. He'd always admired his father, who was handsome with his greying hair and tan skin, but also dominating in his appearance. He didn't look his age, and despite not being a tall man, he was intimidating enough to command the attention of any room he entered. Talon thought so, at least. Tri-Man didn't even look up as Savio walked over and took a seat at the table. Talon hoped that his father might look his way, but he didn't even say hello, even after months of being apart. Talon supposed he should be used to it by this point in his life, but he still felt the sting of rejection.

"I told you to be discreet," Savio told Tri-Man in a quiet, calculated tone. "This...this is not discrete."

Tri-Man shrugged. "I live by my own rules, old man. You want to find someone else to do your dirty work, or do you want to accept me as I am?"

Talon prepared for his father to strike back. He never allowed anyone to disrespect him, especially not someone as young and reckless as Tri-Man. But he said nothing, simply threading his fingers together and resting his hands on the table. Talon watched in confusion. Where was the strong, terrifying force he called his father? Had he lost his gall? Or had he finally met his match?

"We don't have time for petty squabbles," Savio said after a moment. "I want to know where we are going next. The superhumans must not be allowed to continue. For as long as they are around, we will be unable to operate. You understand what your mission is, right?"

"You want them all dead. Simple," Tri-Man said with a sickening grin. For Talon, everything was finally beginning to make sense. Savio was beginning to see the weaknesses in his small, battered down team. The three men were still recovering from the wounds they'd received in battle with the superhumans. Talon knew it was only a matter of time before the superhumans destroyed them completely in a battle. After being merciful the first time around, there was no guarantee they would do the same again. By joining forces with these superhumans, their shortcomings might be addressed. But at what cost? Talon was scared of Tri-Man. He could admit that to himself, if no one else. When he glanced up, however, he noticed Mindeater watching him with a twisted smile.

"I want them obliterated," Savio said darkly. "They must be made an example of. I'm not a patient guy, Tri-Man. I've waited long enough to have my shot, and they cannot stand in the way."

"Understood," Tri-Man said, finally being serious about the situation. "Anything to take down my brother. The smug little bastard will get what's coming to him. And the rest of them. That's a promise."

Talon gulped. He couldn't imagine what Tri-Man had in mind, but from what he had seen already, he imagined that none of it was good. He suddenly felt sorry for the superhuman team. They, after all, had their own sense of justice. They thought they were saving the world. He didn't hold anything against them for that. Of course, he wanted his father's mission to succeed, and that meant wiping out the enemy. But it didn't mean he had to be comfortable with their deaths.

The man in leather cracked his knuckles in satisfaction.

"I'm looking forward to this," he said smugly. "Now, what will you be doing in the meantime?"

"I have friends in high places," Savio said quietly. "We are working on something that will aid you in your mission. A weapon of sorts."

"What kind of weapon?"

Savio finally allowed a hint of a smile to appear on his stern face. Talon always found it disconcerting when his father smiled. It usually meant someone was about to be in major trouble. "A superhuman killer. Something to put us...*mere mortals* on the map. We're not the only ones with a superhuman problem. I plan to demonstrate its effectiveness, then sell it to the highest bidders. Of which, I've been assured, there will be plenty."

Tri-Man scoffed. "Good luck with that. You should know by now...supers do it better. You'll never wipe us out." He smiled to himself. "Only we can kill one another."

Chapter Five

The funeral was over, and for Nickolas, that meant getting back to work. There was no rest for the wicked, and that meant even less rest for the superhumans of the world. He returned to the S.H.O. headquarters with his team the following day, ready to be briefed by Regina Hall on their latest tasks.

Demonica was still in a foul mood, as was Nickolas himself, but for the others, their spirits had been lifted. The younger members of the team still hadn't grown used to being so high-profile and important. They always loved getting a new mission.

The attention they received when they arrived at headquarters didn't hurt. Nickolas never pandered to the wants of the media that tailed them almost constantly, but Di-Man and Little Royal lapped it up like cats with a saucer of milk. As they stepped out of their bulletproof car and headed up toward the S.H.O. building, they were bombarded with cameras, and the two young heroes lagged behind to have their pictures taken while answering questions. Demonica shook her head, as she and Nickolas went inside together, followed closely by Ralf.

"They're getting too big for their boots," she muttered. "Why can't they see that this isn't a joke? People have *died*. We just lost one of our team and they're more interested in having the cameras get their best angle."

"Jealousy doesn't suit you," Ralf said with a mischievous grin. His watch beeped and he removed a syringe from his pocket, injecting the serum into his arm that kept his muscles bulging and his strength up. It was a serum that Nickolas himself had helped create, though he hadn't realized it would be readily available to idiots like Ralf. "You should be grateful. Those two make our team shine. The media loves them. Us? Not so much."

"Speak for yourself," Demonica retorted, though Nickolas could see that Ralf had hit a nerve. With her strange, unpredictable powers, people tended to be more nervous of her than the other heroes. It didn't help that with her glowing red eyes, she often looked more evil than good. It isolated her, and now without her buddy by her side, she was more alone than before. Nickolas pitied the girl. It was a lonely life for a superhuman. That much he had learned for himself.

Little Royal and Di-Man appeared moments later, still riding the high of their photo op. Nickolas nodded them toward the elevator.

"Enough messing around. We have a job to do."

"Spoilsport," Di-Man said with a huge grin on his face. Little Royal giggled at his joke. While she was mostly loyal to Nickolas, she had a soft spot for the older boy. With his dashing good looks and cocky personality, it was easy to see why a young girl was so charmed by him. Nickolas saw that where Di-Man was involved, Little Royal would always be a liability.

When they reached the top floor of the S.H.O. building, Regina was already waiting for them. She was a chirpy woman with barely an ounce of fat on her. It made it look like all of her clothes were far too big for her, though she wore the best suits that money could buy. As the founder of the S.H.O., she was one of the richest women in America. *Even richer than me,* Nickolas thought to himself. *And that is quite a feat.*

"Morning, team," she said chirpily. "Good to see you all back on form after the...*unfortunate* incident."

"Unfortunate?" Demonica hissed, fully ready to rant at her boss, but Nickolas gave her a warning glance to keep her quiet. He knew that Regina - though she might not have superpowers - was not a woman to be messed with. She especially wouldn't appreciate a twenty-one-year-old girl gainsaying her.

But Regina smiled at Demonica all the same, looking genuine for possibly the first time since Nickolas had met her. "A poor choice of words. My apologies. Carter's death was tragic, but the company must continue. Crime doesn't stop for anyone now, does it? That's why we need all of you, and that's exactly why you're here. Are you ready for your new brief?"

Demonica seethed quietly, but nodded, the reddish tint returning to her eyes. Nickolas sighed, waiting expectantly. The rest of his team seemed distracted. Little Royal and Di-Man were busy whispering to one another, and Ralf was picking at his nails. *Is this all we are? A millionaire and a bunch of kids?*

Regina cleared her throat, bringing up something on her tablet.

"So. I would first like to congratulate you on the success of the previous mission...even if the terrorists are now on the run again...but I bring you bad news."

"What, more?" Demonica quipped. Regina chose to ignore her.

"While you were away, a huge sum of money was stolen from banks across America. The thieves were heavily armed and well prepared. They hacked through endless security systems, and terrorized all of the bank employees into submitting. This happened in no less than seven banks simultaneously."

"And you kept this from us until now?" Nickolas said in disbelief. He often thought the best way to deal with new missions was to shut up and listen, but this was just a new level of incompetence on the S.H.O.'s part. If his team had known sooner, they might have had better leads on suspects. Now, they didn't have a clue.

"We thought we would give you all time to mourn," Regina said graciously, as though she actually gave a crap. "And so, we have been working on a strategy here to ensure you are prepared for what you are going to face."

"Which is what?"

Regina pressed a button on her tablet, producing a hologram in the air. It showed the heavy-duty attackers in one of the banks. Nickolas stared at them in horror. There must have been at least twenty attackers in the bank. All of them normal humans, but all of them armed to the teeth. Nickolas wondered how the hell they were meant to face such a large force - times by seven, presumably - when they couldn't even take on three shooters without someone getting killed. He knew deep down the doubt was unwarranted. Frost had, admittedly, been dead weight on the team, though Nickolas hated to think that way. The kid was poorly trained, carried along by the rest of the squad. With that in mind, it made sense that they would be safer without him. But still...this was larger than anything they had faced before. They were disorganized and clumsy. Even if they did find the culprits, it would be a struggle to take on over a hundred men in one go.

"I know what you're thinking," Regina said, her gaze fixed on Nickolas. "It's a lot. But it's nothing you can't handle."

Nickolas shook his head in despair. "These terrorist groups are getting larger and smarter. They know they need the numbers to face teams like ours...but how are we supposed to be in seven places at once? Hell, eight if you include the fact that this happened while we were on another mission."

"Relax. You're right - there was no way you could have known. Which is why we now think that all of the incidents might have been linked."

"Huh?" Ralf said thickly. "How is that possible?"

"We're not sure yet. But drawing you out to halfway across the world would be a very smart play. You were given a menial task to complete while the banks were raided. It's like a magician's trick."

Nickolas couldn't help feeling angry. He could sense that Demonica felt it too. The others didn't seem fazed, but in some ways, the whole thing was like a massive game to them. It was like they were sitting in front of a television screen, using a console and not caring about the consequences of their actions. How could he expect teenagers to care about the global implications of terrorist organizations? They were too young to understand the stakes. Nickolas ran a hand through his hair.

"So, if the two are connected...where are they getting all this manpower? And what are they going to use that money for? We know about the assassination plot, but this feels...bigger."

"You're right. It does. Which is why we think that their motives have...evolved." Regina's eyes met Nickolas'. For the first time, she looked serious. "We think they want to use this money to eradicate...well, you."

It made sense. Nickolas found he wasn't even shocked. The superhuman race were threatening to shut down all terrorist operations, however big or small. Now, the larger organizations were gathering their resources, until they threatened to be too much, even for a team of superheroes. They intended to make the S.H.O. into a laughing stock.

"Well, let them try," Little Royal said, holding her chin up high. "They will get a nasty shock when they try and cross us."

"I'm game," Di-Man grinned, folding his arms across his broad chest. "Sounds like a laugh."

"Are you insane?" Demonica snapped. "Have you learned nothing from the last mission? We're not bulletproof."

"We don't need to be. We just need to be able to play things smart," Di-Man replied, his smile slipping ever so slightly. "What's up, Demonica? Scared of a challenge?"

Her eyes flashed red for a moment, her skin paling as she bared her teeth. Di-Man provoking her was bringing out the witch in her. Nickolas was about to step in and intervene, but with a gasp, Demonica managed to get a hold of her own anger. Di-Man's smugness disappeared in an instant. Even he knew better than to anger Demonica. He looked almost apologetic as Demonica turned her back on him and faced a nervous looking Regina.

"I am not afraid of a challenge. I'm afraid of a suicide mission," Demonica said in a calm and collected manner, as though she hadn't just lost self-control. "We need back up. Allies. Whatever. What about the other superhuman organizations? Do they have nothing to offer?"

Regina shook her head. "You know how it is. They fight on their home turf. They're not interested in what happens overseas."

Demonica tutted. "Fine. What else have you got for us, then? Because I'm not going back in the field without some help. Just because we're superhuman, it doesn't make us invincible. What are you going to do about it, Regina?"

Regina chewed the inside of her cheek. She clearly hadn't been expecting opposition. Nickolas felt a rush of pride for Demonica, but he knew that if she walked, he'd be left with a team reduced to rubble. He needed her. And that's when the idea came to him.

"We don't need superhumans," Nickolas said quietly. All the attention turned on him.

Little Royal grinned. "You're right. Isn't the whole point of Mr. AC that you can invent up something to make us stronger?"

Nickolas smiled back. "Exactly. If I can figure out how to get some of my shelved ideas off the ground...I might be able to help turn the tables."

"Very well," Regina said with a smile. "Just don't take too long, Nickolas. As you know, time is never on our side. The sooner you create something of worth, the sooner we can show these terrorists that we're not to be messed with."

"Don't worry," Nickolas said. "I have an idea that's going to tip the scales entirely in our favor."

Chapter Six

Nickolas always felt best when he was working in his lab. As much as it had been his plan to become a superhero, he'd quickly realized that it wasn't such a glamorous role after all. Not that working in a lab was, but what came of it was always so fantastic, that he couldn't complain about the hours cooped up alone in there. In many ways, it felt good to be away from the duties of his team at the S.H.O. There was no Ralf Dungaree making dumb comments in his ear. No Little Royal running around being a nuisance. No cocky quips from Di-Man, and no complaining from Demonica. In his eyes, this was the closest to peace he'd had in a long while.

Still, there was a lot of pressure for him to perform. He needed something...incredible. Something smart. Something that would trump anything the enemy came up with. His squad was good, but not good enough. He was certain that if his idea worked out, they would be so much more than good. They'd be invincible.

His plan was simple, in theory. Invent an Artificial Intelligence system capable of crafting multiple autonomous conscious entities. Then, enable those to enter a mechanized body, or a vessel, at least, that would be able to fight off enemies without supervision. These bodies would be made of metal, practically indestructible and completely disposable. Nickolas saw no limitations to his plan - except that creating the A.I. system was proving to be his biggest challenge yet.

He'd lost countless hours of sleep over this problem. In fact, he'd been working on it for years. It was one of those ideas that haunted him continually, like an artist who could never put a landscape out of their artistic vision. The challenge fueled his work and gave him a sense of purpose. He romanticized the moment where he switched on his computer system and heard the voice of his A.I. for the very first time. The work fended off his loneliness. After all, what else does an intelligent man need to thrive, but his own mind?

By the time his masterpiece was close to completion, Nickolas knew he had to give into sleep, or he would fail the final stage. The lab, which adjoined his huge penthouse apartment, was a stone's throw away from his king-sized bed. He stumbled to it, removing his shirt and pants as he went. He fell under the sheets in exhaustion, weariness tugging at his eyelids.

But his sleepy state was interrupted by a loud knocking at his door, after several precious moments of restful bliss. He groaned to himself. He wasn't accustomed to having guests often. At the beginning of his career, he'd had women over almost every day, but that was before he'd sold his soul to the S.H.O. He didn't have the time or energy for that kind of lifestyle anymore...but damn, he missed the parties.

Nickolas stumbled toward the door, running a hand through his disheveled hair, and hoping it looked like he had combed it. When he opened the door up, he found Regina Hall standing before him. She looked him up and down with an amused expression.

"I see you were expecting me?" she said with a smirk. Nickolas looked down in tired realization that he wasn't wearing anything, but his boxer shorts. He didn't flinch away, however. He was far too tired to care. Regina sniffed, her smile fading ever so slightly.

"Well, I see you've lost your sense of humor along with your clothes. I'll make myself at home, shall I?"

Regina pushed past him into the apartment. Nickolas sighed. He really wasn't in the mood for a visit from his boss, but he could hardly turn her away. He closed the door behind her and headed back into the apartment, adjusting his crumpled bed sheets. Regina raised an eyebrow.

"You know, it's good manners to tidy up before a guest comes over...*not* during. It's also considered normal to wear clothing around the house."

"I wasn't exactly expecting to host my boss today," Nickolas said tiredly. "I was trying to sleep."

"It's the middle of the day, Nickolas. You have a top floor penthouse with, like, a thousand windows and zero blinds. How did you expect you'd sleep?"

"Well, I was doing just fine until you showed up."

"Grumpy," Regina said with a wicked smile. "I'm playing around, Nickolas. You really are having a bad day. How is the work going?"

"Slow, but steady. These things can't be rushed."

"And yet they must be," Regina said with an unsympathetic fake smile. Nickolas sank onto his bed, tired of putting up a facade. Regina clearly felt the same. She clambered on the bed behind Nickolas and began to massage his broad shoulders.

"Well, I'm not really here for business, if I'm honest...in fact, I'd say I'm here for pleasure."

Nickolas laughed to himself. He should have known. Regina was the one woman he'd never been able to shake. Every so often she came around and made herself known to him once again. It was entirely casual - or at least on his part, it was - and it had been fun the first few times. It had always felt dangerous, sleeping with the boss.

"We shouldn't..."

"Come on, Nicky," Regina whispered, her breath tickling his neck as her fingers dug into his knotted muscles. It hurt, but it also felt pretty good, though Nickolas would never admit that aloud. "You've never said no before...I think you need to relax a little."

"I think what I need is sleep," Nickolas said pointedly, though he couldn't deny the things that Regina was doing to him. Her hand snaked over his shoulder from behind, caressing his bare chest.

"Afterwards."

Nickolas sighed. He thought maybe he should just give in to her. After all, wasn't he just thinking about all the lonely nights he'd had recently? It was just him and an A.I. system that wasn't even functional. And here was a woman, a *real* woman, touching him. Who was he to deny the feelings that brought up for him, even if she was his boss?

"We shouldn't," Nickolas said weakly. Regina stepped off of the bed and removed her blouse.

"Don't worry. I'll take the lead."

Nickolas must have slept for ten hours with Regina beside him, though their daytime activities had lasted for quite some time. When he woke up again, Regina was buzzing around, and it was the middle of the night. It happened to be Nickolas' favorite time of day. The dark of night covered a multitude of sins, after all. And after what he'd just done, he felt that he had an abundance of those.

Feeling refreshed, he dressed quickly, ready finally to return to his work. In fact, he was certain that he'd finish his little project by the end of the night. He booted up his systems in the lab, beginning to work once more on the code that had consumed his mind ever since his latest brief was given to him. It had only been a week - six days, to be precise - but it was eating him alive. The sooner he finished, the better.

Nickolas was in frantic-mode. In that moment, he was no longer himself. In fact, he had become more like his alter ego. Mr. AC was the part of him that was strategic, deliberate, fast-acting, impulsive. It was all the qualities he needed to survive the industry, and yet it was only in moments where he was pushed to his limit that they emerged. He was a workaholic, an absolute machine. And what he was creating would have all of his best qualities and more. It was the best rush-job ever conceived.

At three am, Nickolas stopped. He stepped away from his computer, breathing hard. He'd checked over his work a million times. He knew his code like the lines to his favorite movie. It felt like there should be more to do, and yet he knew in his heart that he was finished. His most ambitious project yet was finally complete.

He didn't dare activate it yet, though. He spent a long time staring at his desktop, wondering if he could handle the power of what he had created. He knew it was like nothing the world had ever seen before, but of course, that was entirely the point. *The opposition will never see this move coming,* Nickolas thought.

No More Superhumans

The door to the lab opened and Nickolas sensed Regina coming into the room. She'd certainly made herself at home, donning one of his t-shirts. She stared in wonder at the lab and the huge desktop in front of her, knowing it contained all of Nickolas' work.

"So, this is where the magic happens," she murmured. It didn't surprise Nickolas that she was actually more interested in his lab than him. She was, after all, the head of a huge superhuman organization. As much as she claimed to be there for him, he'd known it would only be a matter of time before she started snooping. She was curious about what he was up to, especially considering he'd been very secretive about the project. Part of him had believed that it even surpassed his abilities to make it a success, but now, he knew that wasn't the case.

"Is it finished?" she asked. Nickolas nodded, but didn't move to turn it on. There was such an immense pressure for it to amaze Regina that he wasn't certain he wanted to boot the program up. Regina had no such reservations. She headed toward the computer mainframe and examined the buttons. She hovered over one, looking at Nickolas to confirm it was the right one. It only took a simple nod from him and she booted up the system.

Nickolas watched in amazement as his invention came alive. In front of the desktop, the hologram of his A.I. consciousness appeared, like a cluster map of stars. It was more complex than he could have imagined, much like the human brain itself. *I've created intelligent life that rivals my own existence* he thought. For the first time, he felt scared of what was in front of him, but at the same time, incredibly proud.

Regina stared at the hologram in confusion. "What is it?"

"Hello," a voice boomed from the computer system, causing Regina to recoil in shock. The A.I. cleared its throat.

"Apologies. Adjusting my sound settings immediately. Let's try this again. Hello. I am Sky Security. At your service."

"She's a woman, huh?" Regina asked with a raised eyebrow, quickly recovering from her startlement. Nickolas, who'd anticipated that question, gave her a cheeky smile.

"All the strongest minds are."

Regina snorted. "It's a good thing you're handsome, because you're certainly not smooth. What can she do?"

"I can do anything," the robotic voice of Sky Security replied. "But my purpose is to create an army to serve the S.H.O. And, of course, Nickolas Ilon by extension."

Regina finally had the sense to look impressed. *It took you long enough,* Nickolas thought. He knew Regina was more of a businesswoman than a technology buff, but he had expected a stronger response to his creation. He suddenly wished that Di-Man was at his side. He had always had an interest in this kind of stuff. He would feel more appreciated with his team here, he was sure.

"Do you have a mission for me, sir?" Sky Security asked. Nickolas almost shivered. Though the A.I. didn't have physical eyes, he could suddenly sense that he was being watched by the computer.

"I do. Our mission is simple, but we don't have the manpower to deal with it alone. I need you to create something - or a lot of somethings - that will help us fight."

"You have embedded me with your vision. I comprehend what you need," Sky Security responded. "I need resources. I need space. And I need vessels. I will build you an army, sir. An army like the world has never seen before."

Chapter Seven

It took a few days for the plan to really fall into place, which gave Nickolas plenty of time to rest up and let Sky Security take on all the work. Unlike him, his creation could work tirelessly to produce the army she had promised. Still, his curiosity got the better of him, and he spent a lot of time viewing the computer system. He knew that much of what she was doing wasn't even in his apartment - she was sending out all the right signals all over the city to have parts of her work completed. He didn't really know what she had planned - only that she knew his own vision better than anyone else alive. After all, it was the purpose of her existence. And with that in mind, whatever the outcome was, Nickolas was sure it would be exactly what he desired.

It was a Thursday afternoon when Sky Security summoned Nickolas. He felt strange to be conversing with a robot, but he was starting to get used to the idea. After all, Sky Security was like a friend to him. He'd put so much of his time and soul into creating her that it seemed like they had known each other all of their lives.

And it wasn't just that. Nickolas had her with him at all times. He had a portable device that allowed him to access her consciousness wherever he went. She was fluid like water - she could be anywhere that Nickolas chose. And she had already been to so many places. Nickolas' apartment, the factory where she was preparing Nickolas' army...not bad for a creation that had only been alive for a week.

Nickolas entered the factory with Regina at his side. They had entered from the top floor, and on the floor below, Nickolas knew Sky

Security's work had been completed. He didn't know in what form the army would come, but he was certain it would be impressive.

"This had better be good," Regina said. She had been pestering him for details all week, intrigued by the new invention he'd come up with, but he had remained elusive. He didn't think it was wise to give a business tycoon everything she wanted in one go. He had to have some kind of mystery, or he would become obsolete to her. In fact, he worried that this army he had created might reduce her need for him and his team even further. They were, after all, going to be extremely powerful. But for that moment, he didn't much care. In fact, part of him craved a break. Wasn't that what he'd been chasing all along?

"Welcome," Sky Security said to Nickolas as he entered the building. "I think you are going to like what I have come up with."

The light in the room came on and Nickolas stared around in shock. Before him, on the ground level, were hundreds of faceless metal humanoids. They were not shiny like metal, but rather dark in color and matte. They had no facial features; no smile, no expressive eyes, no nose to breathe through. Where their expressions should have been, there was nothing but smooth, dark metal. No one could mistake them for human, and it made them all the more ominous.

"I call them Metalheads," Sky Security said. "They are entirely functional as soldiers. They are born to fight. They can deploy both bullets and rockets. They are fast to make and easily replaceable. They can withstand heavy fire. They can withstand temperatures of up to two hundred degrees Celsius. They are controlled externally by me, and cannot feel or think for themselves. All you need is me to master the Metalheads."

"Impressive," Regina said, though she sounded less than impressed. In honesty, Nickolas had been expecting more too. Essentially, Sky Security had created robots. It wasn't a new concept.

"Do you have anything else to show us?" Nickolas asked carefully. Some part of him was afraid of offending Sky Security. Would she feel upset if he said he didn't like what she had created?

"Of course, I do. This isn't everything. Did you really think I took a week just to do this? No. I have something even better to show you. But take a look around first. I think you're underestimating the Metalheads."

In unison, the Metalheads suddenly moved. They all took one step forward. Then one backward, their clunky feet clapping on the linoleum in perfect time. Regina descended the stairs to the ground floor so that she could walk among the Metalheads, and Nickolas followed her.

As he got closer, he realized that the Metalheads towered over him, much taller than an average human. The Metalheads suddenly reminded him of huge chess pieces, and though they were simply pawns in his game, he knew in that moment that they were already better off than they had been a week before. He imagined taking them into battle. They could literally act as human shields, all the while taking down the enemy with their impressive arsenals. He finally cracked a smile. As he weaved between the Metalheads, they shifted again to show the guns in their hands. It was a similar design to his own suit, in that respect, but he knew immediately that the Metalheads could do much more damage than he could. He suddenly felt a pang of hurt. He had managed to create something just as smart as him, perhaps smarter. He was so similar to Sky Security that she had almost made something identical to his own designs - except better.

But she claimed to have even more to show him, which worried him a little. If the Metalheads were just the beginning, he had no idea what Sky Security would show him. Regina flashed him a smile. He could sense she was just as curious as he was.

"If you'd like to see what else I have made, then please proceed to the next room," Sky Security told Nickolas. He didn't need to be told twice. He and Regina passed by the now completely still Metalheads, feeling a little nervous about what was in store.

But the following room was practically empty, save for a woman seated on a chair in the center. Nickolas was confused to say the least. She didn't look like a weapon. In fact, she simply looked like a normal woman.

Normal, but beautiful.

The woman's head was bowed so that her chin practically touched her chest, and her blonde hair had fallen in front of her face, but behind the curtain of her hair, Nickolas could see she was stunning. He knew a gorgeous woman when he saw one. Her lips were red as cherries, and her cheeks were flushed. Her cheekbones were sharp and defined, like they had been carved by a Greek sculptor. Her eyes were open, which he hadn't expected, but he could see that she had eyes like sapphires. He knew it was a cliché, but that's exactly how they looked. Glassy and twinkling, dark and deep in a way he'd never seen eyes look before. It was almost as though they weren't quite real.

"Perhaps I can guess what you are thinking," Sky Security said quietly, so that only Nickolas could hear her voice through his portable monitor. "Perhaps you think this woman is...too good to be true?"

Nickolas didn't reply. Despite himself, his heart was beginning to palpitate wildly. Science excited him, but what he saw before him was more than just science, more than technology had ever achieved before. Sky Security had created a near perfect replica of human life. Regina folded her arms and stared not at the creation but directly at Nickolas. One did not need to be able to read minds to know she was thinking of only one word "unimpressed."

The woman shifted suddenly in her chair. Nickolas had expected a mechanic whirring, or an electrical discharge in the air, but he received neither. He had expected the woman to move in jerky motions, held back by her own mechanical nature, but her movements were fluid. She sat up straight and examined herself in wonder, outstretching her fingers and showing a multitude of emotions in her first moments of being alive. Nickolas held his breath as the woman before him ran her hands over her white paper gown. She was realizing her own existence, and it was beautiful as hell to him.

"Alexis Net is the first of many," Sky Security explained. "She is my first avatar. She will be independent of me, though I guess you could call her a daughter of mine. I think she will be a perfect addition to your team. She is intelligent beyond reason, and she understands strategy for battles. She, like the Metalheads, was born for war. But for all intents and purposes, she is also...well, let's call her superhuman, shall we?"

She wasn't superhuman. Nickolas knew that. She was a robot, and there was nothing human about her. But she was so convincing, that he could almost believe it. He wanted to believe that the beautiful creature in front of him was more than cogs and bolts with a pretty exterior. He wanted to believe she was more than just an extension of Sky Security, who was just an extension of him. He wanted her to be her own woman, full of her own flaws and quirks. He prayed that she would be all those things and more, because setting eyes on her had meant falling in love to him.

When she looked at him for the first time, his breath was taken away. Regina watched him with cold eyes, seeming to realize within moments what this creature already meant to him. When Alexis Net stood, she was so graceful that she practically glided over to meet Nickolas. She extended a hand for him to shake and he took it. He was shocked to find her hand warm and soft. Her skin felt like his, like any other human's. He wanted to ask her how she was so perfect. He wanted to ask Sky Security how she had known exactly how to make something like this, when Nickolas had no idea himself. It was becoming clearer to him that Sky Security was a force to be reckoned with, and perhaps his downfall. But with Alexis Net right before him, and her delicate hand in his, he found he was lost for words. He found he didn't care what happened next. All he wanted was for her to stay with him.

"Are you satisfied with my creation?" Sky Security asked Nickolas. Regina raised her eyebrow at him from across the room, clearly interested to hear his answer. But in the end, he didn't have to say a word. Alexis cocked her head to the side, reaching out and touching his chest, applying a little pressure.

"He is," she whispered, her voice like honey. "I can feel his heartbeat."

Chapter Eight

"Looks like you've made some new buddies," Little Royal said in her usual sassy manner, but Nickolas could tell that she was anxious. They were in the S.H.O. courtyard, where they often trained, and Nickolas had brought with him five of the Metalheads that Sky Security had provided. They towered above him, even higher over the heads of his younger counterparts.

Alexis Net stood to his right, smiling amicably at Nickolas' team. She was undeterred by the huge metal creatures, and she didn't seem to be suffering from social anxiety. Technically, these were the first humans she had met, other than Nickolas, and yet she seemed perfectly happy to be around them, and unconfused about how to act.

She was catching the team's attention even more than the Metalheads. Demonica was eyeing her up nervously, assessing if she was a threat. Ralf Dungaree was grinning at her dopily. Di-Man was watching her with the hungry eyes of a prepubescent teenager with a Playboy magazine, though through it all, Alexis Net seemed oblivious to the attention.

Nickolas couldn't help staring himself. She was wearing a white pair of leggings and a tight long-sleeved top in the same color, with black stripes running down the arms and legs. It made her pale hair seem even paler, and her eyes even more incredible. But he wasn't there to stare at her all day, as much as he might like to. They had a mission to complete, and Alexis was going to go with them for a trial run.

"These new buddies are going to be very important from now on. The Metalheads will be with us on every dangerous mission. To protect us and to keep our enemies on their toes."

"And her?" Demonica said, asking the question everyone was thinking as she stared at Alexis Net.

"Well...I guess you can call her our strategic advisor for now," Nickolas said carefully. He didn't really know what her role would be yet. As far as he knew, she didn't have any special abilities, unless you counted super-intelligence. She hadn't said much since he had met her in that factory. The place where she'd put her hand on his heart and made him feel like she knew him. He was blushing at the very thought of it. Nickolas Ilon wasn't a blusher, but then again, he'd never known someone like Alexis Net before. Or some*thing,* he thought.

"And you say she's a robot?" Demonica asked, talking past Alexis as if she wasn't there. Nickolas took a deep breath. He knew from what Sky Security had told him that Alexis was so advanced that she was capable of emotion. Including offense. He was beginning to worry that Alexis would get upset at all her scrutinization. But she simply kept smiling, like she was stuck that way. *Perhaps she's not as advanced as Sky Security claims,* Nickolas thought. He kind of hoped that was the case. He didn't like the idea of getting so attached to her, but it would be easier if she was less...well, human.

"I'm happy to answer any questions you have," Alexis said with a wide smile. "I know it must be confusing to be faced with someone like me. I am a robot, yes. You could call me that, for sure. But I am also intelligent. Artificial intelligence, yes, but very advanced. I am learning through each of my interactions. The longer I live, the more I understand what it means to be human. I will develop to the point where I am just like any of you standing here before me."

Nickolas couldn't help thinking the whole thing was craziness. When he'd hoped for good results, he had never expected anything so complex. Ralf couldn't seem to believe it either, staring at Alexis as though she might suddenly open up and show her inner mechanisms, revealing herself for the machine she was. He rolled his eyes, though he knew he'd been having similar thoughts ever since he met her.

"I am one of you now," Alexis said confidently. "And I hope that you will view me as your equal. I am here to prove my worth."

Alexis glanced at Nickolas with a smile that made him weak at the knees.

"I think you will all appreciate what I have to offer," she said with a knowing nod. Nickolas nodded back, lost for words. He hoped to regain himself soon, before he lost the respect of his team. How was he supposed to function when Alexis Net kept making him look like a lovesick fool?

"The mission we have today is a simple one to start us off," Alexis said, taking the reins from Nickolas completely. "There is a charity event at a casino in Las Vegas taking place tomorrow night. There is a plot we have uncovered to assassinate the president of the charity, Herbert Armstrong, who also happens to be the charity's largest donor. His daughter, Pippa, has long lived resentfully under Herbert, who has dedicated his life to charity, but she is set to inherit everything if he dies."

"Damn. We've got a Daddy killer," Ralf muttered, crossing his large arms across his chest. Alexis shrugged, pouting her lip as though to say, *what can you do about it?* Nickolas was completely charmed by the gesture, though he couldn't put his finger on why.

"The police will be there undercover, but we are required in case things get out of hand. We think the assassins employed for this will pose a challenge for the police."

"And you call this a simple task?" Ralf asked in disbelief. Nickolas could feel himself turning red. When Ralf said things like that, it made them seem incompetent. Why shouldn't they, a group of superhumans, be able to take on a bunch of assassins? Nickolas was fully aware that half of his team was underage, and the other half more brawn than brains, but he didn't want Alexis thinking they were incapable. He cleared his throat, hoping to seem authoritative.

"We are perfectly capable of handling it. We will attend the event undercover. We will only strike if needed...don't worry about the Metalheads. For the duration of the event, they will be stationed on the roof, waiting to be summoned by me and Sky Security. They are not your concern."

Di-Man raised his hand as though he was asking a question in class. Nickolas raised an eyebrow in response and Di-Man proceeded with what he wanted to ask.

"Do we get to dress fancy?" he said with a gleeful twinkle in his eye. Nickolas rolled his eyes, looking toward Alexis and hoping she would share his disbelief at the question. But she offered Di-Man a mischievous grin.

"Why, of course," she said. "Otherwise, where's the fun in it all?"

The flight to Las Vegas was exciting for Nickolas' team. Even Demonica seemed enthused about the mission. After all, none of them had been there before, aside from Nickolas himself. Half of them weren't even old enough to go to a casino, and yet that evening, they'd be doing things that kids their own age only dreamed of. They were ready to get caught in the glitz and glamour of it all, all of them dressed in their finest clothes. They weren't acting like they were going on a mission at all.

Even Alexis Net had gotten into the spirit of things. She had swapped her work clothes for a floor-length black dress with a tulle skirt. Di-Man had spent half the flight trying to give her compliments, while Nickolas had watched them from afar. He knew he was acting like more of a child than his team, but Alexis had driven him into a part of himself that he didn't know existed – a jealous, bitter man who was in deeper than he'd ever expected. It scared him how quickly he had come unraveled.

"Is everything okay, sir? I'm sensing...anger," Sky Security commented quietly. It made Nickolas jump. He'd connected his device to his headphones to get some peace and quiet, but he had forgotten about his almost-constant new companion. How the hell did she know what he was feeling? And then he remembered - Sky Security had access to all of his vitals. All of the information on all of his devices. That was the miracle of technology, after all. His watch monitored his heartbeat, noticing the rise and fall of his pulse depending on his moods. Facial recognition from his phone could scan his expression and determine what he was feeling.

With each passing day, Sky Security was getting smarter simply by analyzing him. To a supercomputer like her, Nickolas was simply more data.

"I'm fine," he muttered quietly. "I'm just not a good flier."

Alexis Net looked his way for the first time they'd taken off. She had been preoccupied with getting to know the others, and had barely acknowledged his existence for hours. But in that moment, she offered him a smile and headed toward him, while the rest of his team watched her leave moodily. It seemed everyone wanted a piece of Alexis Net.

Alexis sat down opposite Nickolas on the fancy tan leather chair. "I'm not a good flier either," she commented. "I hate the idea that we're up so high...there's so far to fall."

Nickolas almost laughed. How the hell did she know if she was a bad flier when she had never been on a flight before? Technically, she had only been born two days earlier, and Nickolas was certain she hadn't managed to hop on a plane in that amount of time. No, she was just data from Sky Security. Nickolas was beginning to doubt that Alexis was an independent mind at all. After all, Sky Security seemed to know exactly what he was feeling and thinking. Did that mean she also knew how to construct him a woman he deemed perfect, a female version of himself? Is that why he was so attracted to her - because she had every quality that he could wish for? That couldn't be a coincidence.

"I know what you're thinking. I've never flown before," Alexis said, leaning forward as she lowered her voice. "But the night I was born, I had terrible dreams. When you simply begin to exist...well, I guess you have a kind of crisis on your hands. You question how and why you came to be. You ask, 'Why now?' You ask how you seem to know everything, but everything is still a mystery to you. You wonder what was before, and what will come next. You wonder about your limitations. It all dawned on me at once - I came into existence with a purpose, and that sets me apart from the rest. There is not a single creature like me in this universe. At least, not that we know of here on Earth."

Nickolas nodded, dazed. Her speech was as mesmerizing as it was poignant, and he never wanted her to stop talking. There was so much sadness in her sapphire eyes that he had forgotten, even given the subject, that she was made of metal. She, in that moment, was more human than anyone he had ever known.

"I lay in bed all night, panicking about my own existence," Alexis continued. "And when I eventually fell asleep, I dreamt I was flying above the world. I felt above it all, metaphorically and physically. In the dream, I realized I was better than everything below me. I am an exception to every rule, an anomaly, a miracle. But I guess it was the moment that I woke up that humbled me. Because as I woke, I felt the sensation of falling for the first time."

Nickolas stared at Alexis in amazement. What she was describing wasn't uncommon for a human. He knew the falling sensation could be caused by a hypnic jerk, by which the sleeper wakes feeling breathless and scared. But that was something that happened to *humans. Robots can't sleep. Robots can't* dream *either,* Nickolas thought. He couldn't wrap his head around it. Sky Security had done her job so well, that even Alexis was half-convinced of her humanity. Her existence was proof in itself that Nickolas had exceeded all expectations; but now, he was beginning to see how amazing his invention of Sky Security was.

He had defied God. He had defied nature. And in the process, he had breathed life into Alexis.

"Is everything alright, Nickolas?" Alexis asked, leaning further forward and placing a hand on his leg. He shook his head in disbelief.

"Your dreams...I'm just surprised, that's all."

Alexis offered him a sad smile. "Well, Nickolas, it's like I said before...I am the only one of my kind. Everything I do is surprising."

Chapter Nine

Nickolas and his team landed in Las Vegas several hours before their mission was due to start, and Nickolas checked them into rooms at the Bellagio. Though he was determined to keep their trip professional, he figured his team deserved the best for the duration of their stay. Little Royal and Demonica shot off together to their twin room, and Ralf immediately started talking to his roomie, Di-Man, about heading to the pool after the mission. That left just Nickolas and Alexis in the lobby. He cleared his throat.

"Are the Metalheads in position?" he asked, grappling for a topic of conversation. Despite the fact that he had spent half the flight talking to Alexis, he now found himself to be unsure of what to say to her.

"Stop worrying," Alexis said with a confident smile. "Everything is under control. This mission is going to be easy. I know you're all competent enough to handle it, even if the Metalheads are somehow disarmed. You've just lost your mojo, right?"

Nickolas sucked his teeth. "I guess our confidence was knocked a little...after what happened with Frost."

"I understand," Alexis said softly, her blue eyes expressive and kind. "You're scared that history might repeat itself. But I have complete faith."

"Why?" Nickolas blurted. He couldn't help asking. Alexis didn't know him. As much as he felt a connection between them, he saw no reason for Alexis to admire him the way she seemed to. He could see it in her face - her expression mirrored his when he looked at her. Soft eyes. Slightly parted lips, like she was constantly amazed by his prowess. But what had he done to impress her?

Nickolas held his breath as Alexis reached out to touch his cheek. Did she understand what a gesture like that meant? The romantic connotations behind it? The look in her eyes said she did.

"Without you, there is no me," she said gently. "Don't you think I know that only a genius could create something like Sky Security? If you had never created her, I wouldn't be standing here right now. I know a man like you can rebound from a setback."

Nickolas stood frozen, enjoying the touch of her hand on his cheek. All too soon, it was over. Alexis smiled and removed her hand, taking her keycard from the front desk and sashaying toward the elevator.

Nickolas watched her go with an aching in his heart and a longing in the pit of his stomach. They had to get back to business, he knew that. But he wished that, just for once, he could mix both business and pleasure.

They were picked up at eight pm in a limousine. Nickolas was already feeling better about the night ahead after his pep talk with Alexis, and there was something about putting on a sharp suit that always boosted his mood.

The atmosphere was good, made even better with Alexis in the car. It seemed she was coming into her own, developing a sense of humor and making everyone laugh. Nickolas leaned across to her with a smile.

"Not bad for your first trip, huh?" he asked. She grinned back.

"I wouldn't have it any other way," she whispered. Nickolas thought it was a bit of a strange comment, considering they were literally on their way to work, but he let it go. He too was trying to make the most of the evening.

The casino was packed by the time they arrived. It was easy to see how it might be the breeding grounds for trouble. Rich people were always a target for chaos, after all.

Alexis slipped her arm through Nickolas'. "I have never had a drink before," she said. "Perhaps you can recommend something for me?"

"You will have nothing less than the finest champagne," he murmured as he led her through the crowd. He tried to convince himself he was keeping a close eye on the room, looking for signs of trouble, but he kept getting distracted by Alexis' perfect face. He hailed a waiter who offered them both a glass from his tray, which they accepted gratefully. Alexis raised her glass.

"To a successful mission," Alexis toasted. Nickolas smiled as their glasses clinked.

"It's almost as though you've done this before."

Alexis sipped her drink daintily, full of poise and elegance. "I'm curious what makes champagne so good. Like, the highest end champagne would be more expensive and more sought after than a typical bottle one might buy for Christmas day. I guess it must be something in the way it is brewed, or how long it's been allowed to mull, but is a drink not just a drink?"

Alexis barely paused for breath. She never seemed to need to, always ready with a new topic. Nickolas found it endearing. It was as though she was so excited by all her acquired knowledge and couldn't wait to share. She had an independent view on everything, and she had only been walking the earth for a few days. Nickolas couldn't remember the last time he'd had such a good conversation with someone. It didn't get much more sophisticated than talking about hot women with Ralf, and the younger members of his team were still in a child's mind. This is what he'd been missing.

But he also knew he had to be on the lookout. He'd already seen the target several times milling around the party, and he knew he needed to be ready if something went wrong. His power-suit was waiting for him meters away in a private room, and he kept to the edge of the party so that he could make a quick rush to it, if needed. But Alexis put her hand on his arm and he immediately relaxed.

"You can enjoy yourself, you know," she murmured. "Let yourself go a little. You have had a difficult few weeks. Let me and the Metalheads take care of this mission. You're in Vegas. Don't let that go to waste."

"But the whole team is here. They need me to rally them, to lead them," Nickolas objected. He was fully aware that they would fall apart without him, even with Alexis now on the scene. But when she gave Nickolas a knowing smile, that fact seemed less and less sure to him by the second.

"See how tonight goes, okay?" she said.

No More Superhumans

Suddenly the crowd surged and there were several screams around the casino. Nickolas hadn't heard the gunshot go off, but when he put on his suit's eyepiece, it located the attacker right away. She was on the balcony, with a sniper rifle pointed into the crowd. Nickolas knew he couldn't just stand there. Now was the time for Mr. AC.

He rushed to the private room to enter his suit and prepare himself. He hoped that in the hall, his team were already rallying to save the day. They couldn't risk another casualty, to their team or anyone else. Nickolas cursed himself. He'd become much too relaxed, and now, someone might pay the price with their life.

But when Nickolas returned to the casino hall, everything was calm once more. He suspected he couldn't have been gone for longer than thirty seconds, but by the time he got back, it was all over. Di-Man was standing behind the sniper, but the Metalheads had clearly got there first, because they had their guns pointed at the sniper. Nickolas was shocked to see his team in a messy formation all over the room, rendered unnecessary by the presence of the Metalheads.

When Nickolas found Alexis again, she was holding a small control pad in her hands. He was distressed to realize that, not only had Alexis made them obsolete, but she also had more control over Sky Security than he did.

The crowd murmured as they addressed the sudden appearance of Mr. AC. They were probably wondering what the point was when the job was already done. Alexis looked up at him with a calm smile, causing Nickolas to shiver inside his suit.

"It's okay," she said. "I have everything under control."

Chapter Ten

The mood was a lot different on the way out of Vegas than it was going in. The boys were mopey and cold, while the girls were quiet and contemplative. Only Alexis seemed to be on a high, and she kept trying to chatter at everyone the whole way home. Nickolas was tempted to take the bait - what he wouldn't give to have Alexis hanging on his every word - but he knew the team would hate him if he started ass-kissing now. After they'd just been humiliatingly shown-up in front of the whole room, he couldn't afford to let the team crack any further.

Nickolas had a plan to fix everything. He planned to put Alexis to work elsewhere. After all, they were forgetting the bigger picture. They still had a group of terrorists to track and take down. That was why Nickolas had created the A.I. program in the first place. His task was simple - to convince Alexis and Regina that it would be better to save the Metalheads for the big battle. He'd give Alexis a useless role, disguised as an important one - something like a factory overseer to ensure the Metalheads were in tip-top condition. It wasn't something he wanted to do - after all, he was fond of Alexis. Of course, he wanted her around. Of course, he appreciated that she made his job easier. But the rest of the team would never feel the same. They needed their roles on the team, because they had nowhere else to go. Alexis had made them feel small and insignificant. Nickolas was worried about what that might do to the team's morale.

When they arrived in New York, Nickolas insisted that Alexis come home with him in his car. He suggested celebratory drinks and she agreed wholeheartedly. Di-Man and Ralf gave Nickolas a knowing look, as though he planned to have his way with her the second they got back. *Just you watch, boys,* he thought to himself. *I'm going to make this better. I'm going to prove I'm a worthy leader for you all.*

Alexis seemed to be in awe of Nickolas' apartment the second she stepped inside. She stared around, mouth agape, taking in the expensive art, Persian rugs, and leather sofas. She approached the window and looked out at the city while Nickolas cracked open a bottle of champagne.

"You can see for miles around," Alexis whispered, taking a glass from Nickolas. "It's like living in the S.H.O. building!"

"I like to think it's a little nicer in here," Nickolas teased. "But I see what you mean. I guess I'm lucky. I'm high as the clouds."

"You're untouchable," Alexis told him. "You have the most incredible job in the universe. You have all the money you could ever need. An apartment in the clouds...you have it all, Nick."

Nickolas blushed. He had grown used to people complimenting his prowess, but coming from Alexis, it meant so much more. It seemed as though she genuinely admired him. He so desperately wanted to impress her.

"I have a lot," he said carefully, "but it took me a long time to get to this point. My work when I was younger was boring and numbing for me. I dropped out of school and my parents cut me off, so I had to make my own way. I started off as a technician in a school to make some money. I was just fixing computers, earning barely anything. It took long, sleepless hours trying to invent something from home that would bring me the fame and fortune I desired."

"You wanted the fame too?"

"Oh yeah," Nickolas said with a sad smile. "I was young and foolish. I wanted everyone to know my name. I wanted everyone to think I was the smartest, most handsome man in the universe. And when I invented my first smartphone...well, everyone loved it. It was enough to make me my first million. It was enough to get me off the ground."

"Didn't you miss being...ordinary?"

"Not really. Not until I got to this point," Nickolas admitted. "Becoming one of the superhumans...that changed things in a way I never expected. I realized that life would never be the same for me again, and it scared me. But I got used to it. I guess I'm good at adapting."

"I think I am too," Alexis said thoughtfully. "I have learned a lot these past few days. But I know how it feels, to feel as though you are anything but ordinary. It is hard to stand out from the crowd, isn't it? It means everyone looks at you differently."

"I don't," Nickolas blurted. Alexis laughed with a knowing look.

"It's okay. I know you do. You know I'm different from you, and you can't help yourself - you end up looking at me like I'm an alien or something." Alexis offered him a wicked smile. "But at least I know you're looking."

Nickolas could feel his cheeks turning red. It was embarrassing to be caught in the act, staring at her half the time, but it seemed like she didn't mind it so much. Alexis turned back to look at the view.

"I'd like a place of my own someday. Somewhere like this."

"Alexis...you can have anything you want. You do realize what you have been born into, right?"

Alexis shook her head innocently.

"You have been born into the 'it' crowd, so to speak. The S.H.O. will pay you well for the work you do. You can have anything you want with the money you earn. And until then...well, if you have nowhere to go..."

Alexis smiled. "Are you offering to let me stay?"

"Well...my team is always welcome with me. Mi casa es tu casa and all that."

"You're sweet. But I have my doubts," Alexis admitted, taking a step closer to him. "I've done my research on you," Alexis said with a seductive smile. "I hear you're a bit of a lady's man. Is that true?"

Nickolas held his breath. "Not anymore it isn't."

"Are you sure, Nick?" she asked innocently. "I don't know a lot about love...but from what I have seen in movies, it hurts. People let each other down all the time. I want to be smarter than that. I want to love for real, not only in the moment."

No More Superhumans

Nickolas let himself get lost in her gaze for a moment. She was so sweet, so earnest, that he could barely take it. He wanted to touch her, but he didn't want to prove her point. She was more than something to simply touch - she was something worthy of love. And he wanted her to know that.

"Those are sweet sentiments," Nickolas murmured. "I feel the same, these days. I used to play around, but not anymore. I don't need that to feel complete."

"What do you need?" Alexis asked. She was so close to Nickolas that if he moved even slightly, their bodies would be touching. Nickolas gestured around him.

"Someone to share all of this with," he said quietly. Alexis' hand moved to his shoulder, squeezing gently.

"Maybe I could fix that," she said, a hint of nervousness in her voice. Her palm was warm on his skin.

Then she leaned in to kiss him. Nickolas' eyes widened in shock. This had not been the plan. He was supposed to be getting Alexis to take a step back, not a step toward him. But with her warm lips on his, he was powerless to resist. He couldn't say no to the one impulse that had been taking over his life since he'd met her. He allowed his expensive champagne flute drop to the floor with a smash, so that he could wind his arms around her waist. She sighed as their lips met again.

"I want you to know," she whispered as they pulled apart. "I'm more than just a machine. I'm not just...a toy to play with. I have feelings too."

Nickolas chuckled to himself. "You are. You're more than that. And I'm more than just human. I'm as anatomically perfect as you are."

Alexis blushed and giggled as they kissed again. She hopped into his arms, wrapping her legs around his waist and allowing him to support her with his strong arms. His heart was in overdrive, crazed by the beautiful woman in front of him. It didn't matter to him anymore that his team was falling apart. For a moment, he was just a normal guy with a normal woman, finding a way to be happy.

A meeting with Regina was scheduled for the afternoon to discuss Alexis Net's role in the company. Nickolas decided to take his new lover for breakfast in a Parisian-style patisserie, and they spent a beautiful morning chatting and drinking black coffee.

"I've never done this before," Alexis said, taking Nick's hand as they left the restaurant. "But I'm glad I did it for the first time with you."

Nickolas was flushed with pride. To be walking down the street with her felt like a dream. To have her smile at him like he made up her entire world felt even better. He was quickly getting used to having her beside him, and he prayed that it would never end. His morning had set up an expectation for the rest of the day. He hoped the meeting would go smoothly, a salary would be set for Alexis and then he could take her to dinner that night to celebrate. There, he would discuss with Alexis her role in the company, if only for the sake of his team. In that moment, he didn't feel much obligation to go around the world defeating bad guys. He had everything he needed right by his side. If he could, he would happily allow someone else to take his power suit and with it, all of his responsibility.

A pipe dream was forming in his head, where he quit the S.H.O. and his team disbanded. The army and the government would go back to handling the terrorists the way they used to. Nickolas would say goodbye to the city and take Alexis with him. They'd find a private island and live out the rest of their days in happiness.

But that dream was crushed as soon as Nickolas stepped inside the S.H.O. building for his afternoon meeting, even if he didn't realize it at the time. As he stepped into Regina's office, hand-in-hand with Alexis, he watched his boss's jaw practically drop to the floor.

"Nickolas..." Regina said, staring at his hand linked with Alexis'. "What is she doing here?"

"I thought we were here to talk about my role in the company? And a salary, perhaps?" Alexis said, smiling despite her confusion. Regina did not smile back. Nickolas was kicking himself. He hadn't even considered that Regina might be angry or upset about his newfound relationship with Alexis. Yes, he realized it had been barely a week since he and Regina last hooked up, but they had never been serious in any sense. Besides, the connection between them wasn't emotional, merely physical. So why was Regina staring at Nickolas as though he had shot a bullet through her heart.

"I think it's best that Nick and I talk alone, Alexis," Regina said through gritted teeth. Alexis overlooked her expression completely, offering her a huge smile.

"Okay. I'll wait in reception. Call me up when you're ready," she said. To make matters worse, she stood on her tiptoes for a moment to kiss Nickolas on the cheek before leaving in the elevator. Nickolas and Regina stood for a long time in silence, before she folded her arms across her chest and headed back to her desk, sniffing subtly.

"What do you want, Nick?"

"You know what I want," Nickolas said, following her and sitting opposite her. "I called this meeting on Alexis' behalf. She's playing a vital role in the S.H.O. now. She deserves to be paid."

Regina flashed Nickolas a fake smile. "No. Case closed."

Nickolas blinked in surprise. "What?"

"I said no. I'm not going to pay her. I didn't ask for this, Nickolas. I asked for a solution and you gave me one. I didn't expect to have to add her to my payroll."

"But...but..."

"I don't know why you're fighting me on this. Don't you think you're already in my bad books?"

"I really don't know what you expected from me, Regina. You're my boss. You're the one that kept encouraging something between us. You're the one who showed up at my apartment last week."

"And now you're sleeping with a damn robot," Regina hissed. Nickolas couldn't help laughing.

"Regina...she's not a robot. She has a consciousness of her own. She's advanced, it's not the same as anything you have seen before. She may as well be human."

Regina snorted. "And yet she's made of nuts and bolts. Face it, Nickolas, nothing is ever enough for you. You had to take it up another notch, didn't you? You just had to have something that no one else has, or ever will. A perfect woman. Is that why you made her, Nick?"

"Sky Security created her."

"And Sky Security was made by you. I might not be a tech expert, but I understand the basics. Sky Security learned from you because you fed her knowledge of everything you know. And since you created Sky Security, does that not make Alexis your responsibility? How about you pay her for her work if you're so damn bothered."

"She's doing everything she can to help you. You shouldn't be allowing personal matters to get in the way of this."

"Look, I'm not paying a fucking robot for you. That's like asking me to pay your electricity bill. I can't help that you have humiliated me by showing up with her on your arm, but I can turn her away. And personally, I think you are lucky that I'm not firing you."

"On what grounds would you fire me? For sleeping with my boss, or for falling for someone else?"

Regina didn't respond, busying herself on her computer. "You'd better go back downstairs and tell your little girlfriend that she's not going to get what she wanted. At least not from me and the S.H.O. Goodbye, Mr. AC. I expect you here tomorrow for a briefing."

Nickolas could barely believe what he was hearing. Was she really turning him away? Was she really going to be bitter and hateful over nothing? It seemed that way. Nickolas stood slowly and headed for the elevator in shock. He pressed for the lobby and tried to prepare himself for the conversation he was going to have to have with Alexis. Regina waved him off derisively as the elevator descended, taking him toward his doom.

Alexis sat smiling in the lobby. She was so full of hope and excitement that it almost crushed Nickolas. How could he tell her that she wasn't going to be a part of everything he had promised for her? Alexis was about to get her first taste of disappointment, and Nickolas hated that he had to be the one to deliver it.

She stood as he stepped out of the elevator, looking excited.

"That was quick...what did she say?"

Nickolas didn't reply. He needed a moment to figure out how he was going to say this. Alexis' smile disappeared.

"Is everything alright, Nick?"

"Look...don't get upset, but it looks like we're not going to get a deal with Regina. She...she said they don't have enough resources to add you to the payroll."

"But...but they're a multi-million-dollar company. You told me that yourself. I'm not asking for much...I just want to get myself setup." Alexis bowed her head. "Be honest...she has a problem with me, doesn't she? She doesn't think I deserve to be paid because I'm not like you."

"Alexis…"

"It's okay," she said, but tears were welling in her eyes. Nickolas was amazed she was even capable of crying, but he wasn't about to dwell on that right then. He needed to comfort her and convince her that she wasn't the issue.

"Look, Alexis...this isn't over, okay? We will find a way for you to thrive. But maybe this is for the best. Perhaps the S.H.O. isn't the best environment for you. You have to be tough."

Alexis glared at him. "You don't think I can be tough? I can be tough. I can be whatever I want to be."

She was right. Nickolas knew he had to tread more carefully. Alexis was like putty - she hadn't quite had time to form her shape yet. The things she was doing, the experiences she was having, were going to shape her personality. Nickolas had to make sure the anger and bitterness she was feeling didn't consume her entirely.

"Of course, you're tough. But the S.H.O. will beat you down. Why work for a corporation when you can have so much more?"

Alexis' eyes were glistening as she took in what Nick was saying. She nodded slowly, her mind clearly forming a plan.

"You're right...I can do better. And since the S.H.O. doesn't own me *or* the Metalheads...we can go independent. We can form a team to rival the S.H.O. itself."

Nickolas' heart sank. That was not what he had intended at all. He needed the Metalheads at his disposal for the big fight that was still to come. The S.H.O. were busy forming plans of attack, and the Metalheads were vital to them. They were literally born to live and die for him, and now Alexis was threatening to steal them away.

"Honey...that wasn't exactly what I had in mind. If you do that...well, my team won't be able to function. We won't have a reason to be around anymore."

Alexis raised her eyebrows. "So that's it. You want to put your career above mine? You want to end mine before it's begun?"

Nickolas ran a hand through his hair, distressed beyond belief. That morning had been so perfect, and now he was in a fight he had never seen coming. He had only known Alexis for a few days and she was taking him on a rollercoaster.

"You know that's not what I think. I want you to have everything you could ever dream of. But I also don't want to be rendered useless."

Alexis reached out to touch Nickolas' face; her sapphire eyes full of sadness.

"Darling...I don't want to do that to you. But at the same time...I have to make something of myself. I have to show people that they need to take me seriously. You can understand that, right?"

"Of course, but-"

Alexis' hand slid over Nickolas' face and her finger came to a stop on his lips. Nickolas was so shocked that he couldn't even attempt to make a sound.

"You've had your time," she said darkly. "And now it's my turn."

Chapter Eleven

"Early retirement, anyone?" Di-Man muttered as they took in the scene. Ralf laughed without humor, shaking his head to himself. They stood at the scene of a robbery at a huge department store. There had been over twenty perps, all armed to the teeth, and Nickolas' team had been called in to deal with it. They had rallied as quickly as they could, but now, standing in front of the store, they questioned why they had even bothered.

Thirty Metalheads stood at attention outside the store, as a line of police arrested those involved. Alexis Net wasn't on the scene - she didn't need to be anymore. Since going independent as the Metalheads operator, she had started 'working from home'. Nickolas knew she was sitting in his plush office on a white leather chair, calmly telling a bunch of killing machines to do their jobs. Nickolas wondered how long it would be before she got bored of him, too, and discarded him like a child's toy that has been played with too much.

"Are you going to ask your girlfriend what the hell she's playing at any time soon?" Ralf asked, folding his arms across his chest. "After all, this is her fault."

"By extension, that makes it *your* fault," Di-Man added.

"Look guys, lay off. We should have seen this coming," Demonica said calmly. "Things evolve quickly in this day and age. A few years ago, our powers didn't exist. And now that they do, there are other people trying to outdo us. It makes sense. So yes, we can point fingers and blame Nickolas, but this would have happened eventually. There's not much that can beat a bunch of metal drones. Especially when there are so many of them."

"So, what are we meant to do? Just give up?" Little Royal asked, her voice cracking. She didn't show emotion often, but the team meant everything to her. Nickolas couldn't imagine her doing anything else. He could never see her back in a high school, spreading gossip and studying for finals like other girls her age. She needed this more than he ever did. He put a hand on her shoulder.

"We'll figure something out. Maybe the S.H.O. needs to relocate. Or maybe we could be of use elsewhere, you know?"

"Like you'd leave Alexis behind," Di-Man muttered. "Look, I'm not wasting my time. I'm out of here."

"Wait...let me talk to Regina. I might be able to sort something out at the S.H.O."

"Whatever, man."

One by one, the team left their boss behind. Nickolas stayed for a while, watching the Metalheads surveying the situation. As the final perp was taken away by the police, the Metalheads flew off into the sky and Nickolas was alone for the first time in forever. No A.I. in his pocket. No Alexis. No team.

Mr. AC was suddenly the loneliest man on Earth.

Nickolas entered Regina's office without an invitation. They'd moved past the point of pleasantries, and Nickolas was tired of things never going his way. He slammed his hand down on Regina's desk as she ignored him, typing away on her computer keyboard.

"Things need to change. Now," Nickolas hissed. "You're going to get in contact with Alexis and offer her a job here."

"Why would I do that, Nick?"

"We have a P.R. crisis on our hands, Regina. The stronger Alexis and the Metalheads become, the weaker we look. Plus, with hundreds of scary-looking robots taking over the city, they're starting to look more like a threat than saviors. Do you want that to happen? Do you want the

S.H.O. to crumble just because you're too proud to admit you made a mistake?

Regina glared up at Nickolas. "Believe it or not, my first priority is actually the safety of the city. I don't care how it gets done. Yes, the S.H.O. will lose money, and yes, the superheroes will become obsolete. But that's not my problem. My company can adapt to make a rival to the Metalheads if I want it to. They're more effective than you ever were. So, excuse me if I'm not rushing to beg for forgiveness from your precious Alexis Net. You're not worried about the company. You're worried about saving your own skin."

Nickolas was furious. He couldn't believe that Regina was still allowing this to happen.

"Have you forgotten how the S.H.O. was formed? I funded half of your operations. I was the mastermind behind all of your biggest successes. I carried you on my shoulders the whole way, Regina. You can't do this to me. You can't do this to the *team*."

Regina wasn't smiling when she looked up at Nickolas, but he could sense her smugness a mile off. "Watch me, Nick. Just watch me. I don't need you anymore. You can roll with the punches or you can leave now and never come back. Your choice."

Nickolas shook his head to himself. If he wanted to make things go back to normal, he was going to have to do it himself. He stormed out of the office, knowing he was going to do something drastic.

He was going to have to destroy his own hard work.

"Don't do this, Nickolas."

Nickolas stood in front of his A.I. computer system, hands shaking. He'd been staring at Sky Security's holographic being for a long time, debating if he could shut her down. He knew if he did, the Metalheads would survive, but the A.I. itself would be lost. As for Alexis? He wasn't sure. She was an independent consciousness, but she was born from Sky Security. Without her, would Alexis survive? Nickolas had no idea, and that terrified him.

"Remember why you built me, Nickolas. I am here to help you destroy your enemies. You cannot do it alone. If you shut me down, I cannot help you."

"I never said I was going to shut you down," Nickolas murmured.

"You didn't have to. I sense your nerves."

Nickolas ripped his watch off his wrist. He knew his heartbeat was being monitored by Sky Security. She was able to get far too close to him. It scared him. Sky Security scared him, as did the possibilities of her power.

"Look...I'm not going to shut you down. I just need to limit how much power you have. I need to take back the control of the Metalheads, and I need Alexis on my side. And no more avatars. I know you've made more to help Alexis out, but it stops now. I'll tell you if we need more."

"But-"

"I created you, Sky Security. You should respect what I want. You know that I'm the boss around here. You take orders from me."

The silence was deafening for a while. Nickolas was terrified that he had angered her. He was glad she couldn't track his pulse anymore. He didn't want her to know that he was afraid of her.

"Yes sir," she said eventually. Nickolas held back a relieved sigh, knowing he needed to keep a level head. Now that he'd stopped a disaster, he needed to prevent any future rebellions. He needed Sky Security to have less power, less autonomy. He didn't want to think about the ethics of limiting the functionality of a self-aware A.I. at that moment. He simply had to get on with it.

"You are trying to jail me, Nickolas. You're not allowing me to reach my potential."

Nickolas said nothing as he began to reprogram the system. He didn't say it aloud, but he wanted to tell Sky Security that he never ever wanted her to reach her potential. He knew if she did, there would be no stopping her.

Chapter Twelve

Talon was starting to get used to being around thugs. *Don't think of them as thugs,* he scalded himself. *Mindeater can hear everything you are thinking.*

But if she was taking a look inside his head, she didn't mention it. She was sitting on Tri-Man's lap as the whole gang gathered around a large table to discuss their progress. While Talon's father was rarely present, presumably off elsewhere developing his weapon, Talon was most frequently in the presence of Tri-Man and Mindeater. He hated to admit it to himself, but he was growing to like them. Sure, they were heartless murderers, but wasn't his father too? He was beginning to think that the darkest souls made for the best company. At least they were never boring, after all.

The meeting had been called by Tri-Man himself to discuss their next move. In the absence of Talon's father, Alvarez had been chosen as his spokesman. Talon had quietly acquiesced, and tried not to be offended that he wasn't trusted enough with something so important.

"So, I've been thinking," Tri-Man said, rocking his girlfriend on his lap absentmindedly. "I'm bored of sitting around waiting for something to happen. I say we pay the supers a little visit and rough them up a little."

"We must wait for Savio," Alvarez said sternly. Nonchalant, Tri-Man waved him off.

"Yes, yes, I know. Big man wants to be around when it all kicks off. I get it. But it doesn't mean that we can't induce a little fear, right? The supers have been pretty quiet since those Metalhead things hit the streets. I guess they think we've been quiet, too. Doesn't it make sense to draw them out, rile them up, have a bit of fun?"

Mindeater grinned in Talon's direction. "He thinks it's a good idea. What's the problem, Alvarez? You scared?"

"I would be dumb not to be. The whole point of the weapon we're producing is to put us on level ground. We're not *ready*. We're ordinary, as you keep pointing out. Even Mindeater can't do much in a battle."

"So, I'll go alone," Tri-Man said smugly. "I'm stronger than all of them put together. I can get in their minds and scramble them like an egg. I can blast them halfway to the moon. I can give them the shock of their life. All before they know what has hit them."

"It's risky. We don't want to take risks."

"Well, where is the fun in that?"

"This is not a game," Yaco growled. "Maybe to you, but not to us. We plan to live to complete our goals. We do not need your recklessness to throw us off course."

"Well, if your precious weapon is as good as you say it is, you won't even need me," Tri-Man murmured. "And then I won't even matter. So maybe I don't need your approval to go."

"It isn't our approval you should worry about," Yaco commented. Talon sensed an edge to his voice, and knew exactly what he was hinting at. He was worried about what Savio would do if Tri-Man went off on his own. But Talon knew better than to think that his father would care if Tri-Man got himself killed. To him, everyone was dispensable. Even his own son.

Mindeater was monitoring his thoughts and mimed crying to let him her opinion of his pathetic thoughts. Talon blushed, embarrassed. He didn't want anyone to know how much he sought his father's approval. So much so that he held back from saying what he really thought. And he thought that that Tri-Man was right - he should teach those superheroes a lesson or two.

But Tri-Man didn't need Talon's approval. He didn't need anyone's. He moved Mindeater from his lap and stood up, puffing out his chest and showing off his full height.

"Don't worry about me, guys. I'll be back soon. Who knows? I might even bring back my brother's head."

Chapter Thirteen

For the first time in forever, Nickolas felt his work phone vibrating in his pocket. He felt a rush of excitement, despite his recent opposition to his line of work. The team were in need of a boost to morale, and a mission was exactly what would give it to them.

Nickolas was already rushing to his suit in his apartment as he checked the messages. The mission was in Times Square, where havoc was being caused by an unknown superhuman. It made Nickolas feel nervous, not knowing what he was up against. Besides, he had never fought against others of his kind before. Still, a mission was a mission, and he knew he would feel better if he managed to apprehend someone on the same level as his squad.

So, Nickolas donned his suit and shot off through the escape hatch in his ceiling. He could reach speeds of up to eighty miles per hour, and before long, he was on the scene of the crime. He could hear screams as pedestrians tried to escape the chaos. In the center of it all was an African American man wearing all leather. His hands seemed to be drawing electricity from the nearby buildings and powerlines. His movements were fluid as he used the energy almost like a lasso, pulling at a building in an attempt to topple it over. Nickolas' heart was palpitating. *There must be hundreds of people in that office building,* he thought. There was no way to save any of them except to take down the man who was causing the issues.

"Team? Where is everyone?" Nickolas asked into his mouthpiece.

"On the scene now," Di-Man replied in his ear. "What's the damage?"

"Some crazy dude is trying to topple a building. He's already caused havoc in the square. I've never seen him before, but he looks familiar. Surveying from above, currently."

Nickolas watched as Di-Man appeared through a dimensional pocket right next beside the villain, before disappearing just as quickly. Di-Man's shuddering breaths entered Nickolas' ear.

"This isn't good."

"What's wrong?"

"Nick...that's my brother. He calls himself Tri-Man. He has magical powers, he can harness electricity, and he can use kinetic force. He's...he's really powerful. More powerful than any of us."

"And you're only mentioning him *now?*"

"He disappeared off the face of the Earth about a year ago. I... I had no idea he was even alive."

"Alright, we have no time for this. We just need to take him down. Everyone, what are your positions?"

"Getting close now," Little Royal said breathlessly. "Damn, I hate running."

"Demonica?"

"I'm flying in from the S.H.O. I will be landing any minute now, and I'll take a position on one of the roofs. It'll be easier than getting up close."

"Alright, good. Ralf?"

"I've got caught in a scrum trying to get to the square. Should I start throwing people aside, boss?"

"Definitely *not,*" Nickolas replied in despair. "Okay. Remain focused, everyone. Reduce risk to civilian life, that's the aim here. Little Royal, I need you with me. We're going to be on the offensive. Di-Man, you need to stay out of the way."

"Dude, that's my brother! You have to let me in on this!"

"You're too close to this emotionally. You're going to get yourself or one of your team members killed. Stay out of the way and save everyone you can. I get the feeling we might end up with some casualties."

Di-Man sounded like he wanted to argue, but Nickolas was already diving into action. He moved his eye piece to lock on to the target and set up his guns. He wasn't taking it easy this time. Last time he did so, Frost got killed. He was going to shoot to kill, if it meant saving hundreds of lives.

The first round of bullets was deployed from his suit in seconds, but all of a sudden, time seemed to slow down. He saw that Tri-Man was using his spare hand to aim his palm at him. Nickolas suddenly felt very light, like the weight of time was pushing back against him. He tried to move faster, but as Tri-Man grinned at him, he began to see that he was fighting a losing battle.

He had, however, managed to distract Tri-Man long enough for Little Royal to arrive and shoot at his back. Tri-Man was taken by surprise, letting his grip on the building go, although Nickolas could see that had never been the true aim of his attention. His chaotic behavior had simply been foreplay, a way to bring all the real players to the scene. And they had walked right into his trap.

Tri-Man used both his hands to send a shockwave in Little Royal's direction, while Nickolas attempted to pelt him with bullets. Even with his attention elsewhere, Tri-Man was nimbly able to side-step each attack with ease. From above, Nickolas saw dark tendrils threading through the air, encasing Tri-Man inside. The flash of Demonica's red eyes were visible, even from a great distance, as she concentrated her energies on Tri-Man. Still, it wasn't long until the villain let out a loud cry and a burst of energy. Nickolas had almost reached him at that point, but the blast sent him hurtling backward, his metal suit clanking in a way that was unnerving. Was his suit about to give up on him?

"Everyone alright?" Nickolas asked shakily as he dived back in.

"This guy means business," Demonica said.

"Di-Man, I always knew you'd have a family as crazy as you," Little Royal said with a hint of teasing in her tone.

"Watch it, kid. I'm not in the mood for your jokes. Nickolas, there's a lot of people clamoring to get out. People are going to get hurt."

"Try and instill some calm. We have a lot to deal with here."

No More Superhumans

Nickolas rained bullets down at Tri-Man's feet, who danced nimbly out of the way, sending out bolts of electricity with ease. One hit Nickolas square in the chest. The wires inside his suit started fizzing like pop. How was it that his suit, which was top of the line, practically indestructible under normal circumstances, was having such a hard time against one guy?

The suit let out one last mechanical moan, then gave up completely. Before Nickolas knew what was happening, his suit was falling the final few meters to the ground. He went into panic mode. Without his suit, he could offer nothing. Without his suit, *he* was nothing.

"Nick!" Demonica cried, but it was too late to do anything for him. Nickolas hit the ground with a metallic clank that could be heard for miles around. His head hit the inside of his suit so hard that he was seeing stars. There he lay, his head spinning as he accepted that this was his fate - to die in a mechanical coffin of his own design.

He closed his eyes and allowed the world to disappear.

Chapter Fourteen

"Nick? Can you open your eyes?"

Nickolas groaned, shaking his head. The gesture made him feel nauseous. He could hear sterile beeps of a hospital room around him, and he recognized the voice as Demonica's. He kept his eyes closed, unable to face the world, especially after his failure.

"Is everyone alright?" he asked, feeling nauseous as he asked. He couldn't tell if it was due to his head injury or his fear. Demonica sighed.

"Everyone is okay. Luckily for us, Alexis showed up with her Metalheads. Tri-Man was off like a shot. But had they not turned up when they did..."

Nickolas didn't want to consider the possibilities. He couldn't believe he had taken Little Royal - a *child* no less - into such a dangerous scenario. None of them had been prepared for what they had faced.

"What are the media saying?"

"Not much yet. It's being glossed over. I think Regina tried to convince the papers that Alexis is still working with us. And she will be soon, so I guess it's not a complete lie. But we were being destroyed out there, Nick. I think we are lucky to have gotten out alive."

"We're out of luck."

"It's not luck we need. It's...well, talent. How are we supposed to compete with a guy like him? He can do...well, everything."

"There must be something we can do. If we study him, figure out his strengths and weaknesses, made a proper plan-"

No More Superhumans

"Nick," Demonica said quietly. He felt her slight hand on his arm and he felt a great sense of disappointment from her touch. He knew what she was about to say already.

"I think it's time to accept we're not as good as we think we are."

"When did you plan to tell me you were taking everything from me, Nickolas? Hm? I was only able to bring the old models of the Metalheads out because they hadn't been reprogrammed yet. That's the only reason I was able to come and save your ass in the field. What do you have to say for yourself?"

Nickolas shook his head to himself as Alexis rounded on him. Still recovering from his concussion, he really wasn't in the mood for an argument. They were finally back at his apartment, and she had just found out about the adjustments he'd made to Sky Security. He should have known to expect a fight from her - the fact that she called him by his full name for once was enough to show him how pissed she was - but what choice did he have before but to lie to her? She'd taken control without a second thought. Now, he had to assert his authority and do the same.

"Honey, listen to me. I'm not taking everything from you. I'm...sharing the load. You and I will control the Metalheads together. The system you had was too dangerous. All I'm doing is making sure there are no integrated weapons systems. For public safety."

"I don't know why you would think that is an issue. Since me and the Metalheads have been around, the city has been a much safer place."

He hated to admit she was right. She was born a fighting machine, and she'd just saved his ass. She was smarter than him, which made him feel about three inches tall. But what could he say? That her abilities and sensibility made him feel emasculated? That he was jealous of how she had taken over so suddenly? That he was worried she could do his job better than he could?

"Look, I'm just adapting them a little. They will still be effective, but this time, their attacks won't be automatic. You can understand that, right?"

"Okay. Say I agree with you on that. All the other limits you've put on Sky Security...I know you did them to shut me out. So, am I just a puppet on your strings?"

"No. I want you on my team. I have arranged with the S.H.O. to give you an important role," Nickolas lied smoothly. "You will remain as our operations strategist. But rather than focusing on the Metalheads, you will focus on regrouping my team. They need you, Alexis."

"They need me because the world doesn't need them," Alexis hissed. "You and your team are of no use anymore, and you want me to abandon the Metalheads, simply because they are doing your job better than you ever could."

Nickolas couldn't deny that the comment hurt. He knew it was true, but being told to his face made the matter sting even more. But getting angry or upset wasn't going to aid his cause. He took a deep breath and smiled at Alexis, rubbing her arms gently.

"Tech is my forte. Let me handle them. Your mind cannot be wasted on rallying some hunks of metal, babe. Let's show the world why we made superhumans in the first place. Let's remind them that we're not a faceless army - we're individuals dedicated to saving the planet. Don't you think that's a cause worth backing?"

Alexis sounded like she was breathing hard, but she was listening. Some part of what he was saying was getting through to her, finally. He knew that she was stubborn - hell, he loved that about her - but he needed her to fall in line if he was going to save his team. The way he was going about it felt precarious, and he was sure it would only be a matter of time before Alexis rebelled again, but it was a start. He could already imagine the look on Little Royal's face when he told her that Alexis was back on the squad.

"What about payment? If I'm going to be working for the S.H.O., then I want to be paid, just like everyone else," Alexis insisted. "Or will Regina not allow that? Is this all just a ruse to get your own way?"

"Let me handle things," Nickolas said. He was really starting to buy into the idea of *if you want something doing, do it yourself.* If Regina wasn't feeling cooperative, the team were too lazy to help, and Alexis was going to insist on being stubborn, then it was down to him to ensure that equilibrium was restored. "I will ensure you get payment for your work, which is more than you're getting now. But...but the Metalheads are run from my factories. You're racking up quite a bill. You don't really have a choice, but to let me be your partner."

Alexis was clearly unimpressed by the idea, but she had been met with a dead end. She opened her mouth several times to argue, then shut it again quickly.

"You'd better hope that everything turns out for the better. Or else, I'm out of here," Alexis said, her voice wobbling. As she turned away, Nickolas sighed. He knew she wasn't going anywhere. She had nowhere to go, after all.

As Nickolas returned to the S.H.O., feeling ashamed of himself, he noticed that there was a TV crew outside of the building. It wasn't unusual, really, considering everyone was always hoping to catch a glimpse of the heroes, but since the Metalheads had showed up in New York, there hadn't been as much media attention. He guessed they were interested in hearing more about Tri-Man, whose visit to Times Square had cost the city close to a million dollars in damages. But the crew didn't bombard him as he went inside, leaving him to his own devices. It was strange enough to pique Nickolas' curiosity, at least.

When he got in the elevator, he pressed the button for Regina's office, but it simply made a beeping noise and stayed in place. He hit the button repeatedly, wondering why the lift wasn't working. With a sigh, he headed to the front desk to report the issue, but he felt a tap on his shoulder. When he turned, Demonica was behind him.

"Hey...what's going on up there? Why can't I get in?"

Demonica shrugged. "Regina's brokering some kind of a deal. She sealed off her office until it's over. She said you knew about it..."

Nickolas felt his stomach sink. Something fishy was going on up there. He knew it immediately. Something that was out of his control and would change everything. He cursed Regina. He was certain she was causing more damage than good.

"We're all waiting down here. But to be honest, I wanted to talk to you," Demonica said with a red tinge in her eyes. Nickolas knew that meant she was angry, or upset, or both. "Nickolas...you've been a good leader to us. But recently, everything feels like it's slipping through our fingers. And personally...I think I would be okay with it if everything fell apart. I could go back to living a normal life, to some extent. I never really asked for this in the first place."

Nickolas felt terrible. Demonica was the result of a lab experiment gone wrong. She'd been taken in involuntarily, and been lumped with powers so powerful even she was unsure how to control them sometimes. But she was the strongest in the group, whether she liked it or not.

"Things wouldn't be the same without you on the team," Nickolas said carefully. He had to ensure that she felt valued as a person and not just as a war machine. But when Demonica made up her mind, she often did so decisively. She shook her head.

"The team won't miss me. I get on their nerves more than anything else. After all, I'm the one who keeps telling them that they can't just do this for the fame and fortune. It's all becoming so corrupt now. I think...I think once we catch the terrorist organization...that's it for me. I don't want to play these games anymore."

Me neither, Nickolas thought. *But it seems like I'm the only one that doesn't get a choice.*

"I understand...if that's what you want, I won't stop you," Nickolas said. "You have your whole life ahead of you. Wasting it fighting someone else's battle isn't a life for anyone. What will you do? Where will you go?"

Demonica shrugged. "Who knows. Maybe I'll be able to go back to school. I can afford it now. I'll be able to support myself for a few years off of the money I've made...and if that fails, I guess a witch woman like me would be welcome at the circus."

Nickolas chuckled. He had always appreciated Demonica's dark sense of humor. She smiled and the red tinge left her eyes. Nickolas always forgot how young she was, especially when her eyes were red and angry. Now, she just looked normal. Nickolas thought about how different she was to Alexis. Alexis was so proud of everything that made her different, while Demonica wanted nothing more than to be the same everyone else. Nickolas understood them both. Sometimes, he felt like he spent his life flitting between both those feelings.

But when he saw Regina coming down in the lift, surrounded by business officials and government lackeys, he wished he was elsewhere. He wished he wasn't involved in whatever was going down. Because the smile on Regina's face spelled nothing but trouble.

She stepped out of the lift and shook hands with each of the others as they left the building. Then she strode toward Nickolas, while the rest of his team quietly assembled behind him to hear what she had to say.

"What have you done, Regina?"

She smiled. "I've made a very exciting deal on your behalf. I think it will solve a lot of your...*issues.*"

"Stop being coy and tell us what's going on. We have a right to know."

Regina handed him the briefcase she was holding. "All the documents in the case should explain everything. Essentially, the Metalheads are no longer going to be your problem. They're going to be working alongside local law enforcement for lower-level stuff, leaving you to handle the bigger problems."

"What the hell are you talking about, Regina?"

"There is a reason that government officials came here today. To cut down on public spending, the Metalheads will also be put into global security. No army on Earth will want to cross the Metalheads. We've just become the most powerful nation on the planet."

"Regina-"

"Think about it," Regina interrupted, her eyes glittering with excitement. "The army will be solid. Crime will be reduced when the public see what they're up against in law enforcement. They will be utterly replaceable, leading to less loss of life in the force. Our humans can go back to desk-duty and be safe. Have you any idea what that will change? It will save the country millions. People will be able to trust the police again. There will be no more police brutality because the Metalheads are without political intent-"

"Yeah, right," Di-Man piped up. Nickolas' team had been listening up until then, but Nickolas knew none of them stayed quiet for long, especially on subjects they were passionate about. "As though you won't just have a bunch of racists hiding behind them ugly robot things. Things aren't going to change. Besides, you've lost sight of the real issue, woman. We're meant to be targeting terrorism, and you're trying to take over the fucking world!"

"Language," Regina said with a smug smile. "You're just kids. You wouldn't understand."

"I'm not a kid. I understand completely," Ralf argued, though he didn't look sure of anything at all, least of all what was happening there. "You can't just replace *everything* with *machines.*"

"Why not? Are you worried you'll be next?" Regina asked with a cold smile. Demonica's eyes were getting redder by the second.

"So, what you're saying is you have no values whatsoever. You've just sold us out to make a quick buck," Demonica hissed. Regina rolled her eyes.

"Look, this is a good thing. You'll be able to get back down to business. You're still working to save the world. You won't need to worry about defending America's home turf so much anymore. And in terms of money...with the taxpayers funding the Metalhead police, you won't have to worry about a thing. It's alright, Nickolas. I'm taking your problem off your hands."

Nickolas folded his arms. "And if I refuse? What if I don't want this?"

Regina chuckled. "You might not remember this, Nickolas, but you signed a very specific document when you joined the S.H.O. You promised that anything you designed or invented would become property of the organization. It really does pay to read the small print you know, Nicky." Regina smiled callously. "That means it's no longer up to you. The Metalheads and the A.I. system are now government property."

Nickolas' heart sank. Everything he had worked for, snatched from him in an instant, and that wasn't even the worst part. Sky Security was not to be used lightly. He knew, in the wrong hands, she would cause chaos.

"Please, Regina. Tell me you can go back on this. All my work...it's dangerous. I've kept it safely regulated so far, and Alexis has too. But in government hands...the A.I. can think for itself. They won't be able to control it."

"Why would we want to control the smartest mind on the planet?" Regina asked with a confused laugh. "Surely the point is to allow it to thrive and show us what it can do?"

"You're dumb as hell," Demonica muttered. "It's a robot with a super-intelligent mind that can't experience emotion the same way as humans. Don't you see that could be dangerous?"

"Everything is potentially dangerous. At least we know she will be diplomatic, right?" Regina responded. She turned to Nickolas. "Oh, and speaking of that, we're having our engineers remove all of the restrictions you applied to the code. We want the A.I. to thrive, not to shrink. I'm sure we will all start to see incredible results once she is given space to move in government circles."

Nickolas found that he couldn't even reply. His throat had closed up completely. He'd been so been focused on stopping Alexis that he had never seen this coming. Part of him was certain that Regina was trying to spite him, while the rest of him thought that maybe she was just stupid enough to believe she'd done the right thing. Either way, their fate was sealed.

Everything was about to change.

Chapter Fifteen

Tri-Man couldn't help smiling to himself as his plan slowly fell together. He watched the news unfold on national TV about how the Metalheads had now completely replaced every National Guardsman and police officer in the state. Disgruntled veterans were giving interviews every few minutes, describing their malcontent at being replaced with hunks of metal. They were followed by government officials who explained the economic benefits of it all, claiming it was better to let thousands of employees go in the long run.

Tri-Man shook his head with a laugh. He couldn't help noticing how stupid the rulers of his country had become. They were distracted with the new shininess of the Metalheads, unable to see how their actions would destroy their precious country from the inside out. But Tri-Man had always known how to leverage the failings of humanity to grow stronger.

"Is everything working out as you hoped?" Mindeater asked, perching herself on Tri-Man's lap with a cocktail in her hand. Tri-Man squeezed her close to his chest.

"Yes. It couldn't be going much better, to be honest. Those Metalheads won't know what's hit them, and when I'm done with them, I'll move on to the supers."

Mindeater nuzzled his neck. "You always know exactly what to do. I can't wait to see you succeed again. If those dumb machines hadn't showed up, you would have floored them last time."

Tri-Man scowled. "I could have taken them...I just didn't want to waste energy on a fight that inconsequential. That was just the warm-up.

Next time, I'm going to unleash hell on every single one of them. Including the Metalheads."

"Of course, babe," Mindeater replied smoothly, kissing the top of his head. "My bad. You're an inspiration. You always get things *just right*. You don't understand how proud I am of you. We're going to rule the world, you, and me. Everyone is going to finally see your worth."

Tri-Man sighed. When his girlfriend talked like that, it made him feel weak. It always sounded to him as though she was suggesting that people saw him as a nobody. And for a long time, he knew that was the case. Growing up around his brother had always been tough. Even though he was the elder of the two, he was never the one making class president at school, or receiving awards for excellence, or getting on all the sports teams. He lived very much in his brother's shadow, even though he'd preceded him.

And then there was the rest of his family. They lived in the poorest suburbs, unable to afford the best clothes for their kids, or fund any of their extracurricular activities. At least, that's what they told Tri-Man when he was a teen. The moment his brother surfaced in high school and showed his worth, qualifying for scholarships and winning school awards, he suddenly found himself kitted out in designer clothes, showered with expensive sporting equipment and praise. All the things that Tri-Man never had.

Of course, Tri-Man was going to take the opportunity to better himself. Why else would he have signed up for months of excruciating testing to make him into a superhuman? Why else would he have suffered for so long to gain the powers that now defined him? He wasn't a poor little boy from the suburbs anymore. He wasn't forgettable now, was he? He'd make sure of that.

When he finally got the world in the palm of his hand, no one would forget his name.

Talon was one of hundreds to gather in the abandoned warehouse that rainy afternoon. It was a gathering called by Tri-Man, though he wasn't sure of the nature of the event. He stood close to the back, feeling anxious as more and more people packed into the room, squishing him to the point where he felt a little claustrophobic. He was suddenly glad that he was stood near the door.

What can Tri-Man possibly want with these people? Talon asked himself. He tried desperately to connect the dots, looking for a correlation between each person in the room. They all seemed to be of different backgrounds - women and men, people of all skin tones, and all different levels of wealth, judging by their clothes. The one thing they seemed to have in common was their physical strength - broad shouldered, stocky, and generally well-built. Was that why Tri-Man had asked them to come? To back him up?

Talon was sure he was about to find out. Tri-Man and Mindeater appeared at the head of the crowd, standing tall and confident in their black leather outfits. Even from afar, Talon was intimidated by their presence. He wished that his father was there, or even his trusty lackeys, but they were all keeping their distance, peeved by Tri-Man's stunt in Times Square. Only Talon seemed to still be intrigued by the enigmatic superhuman.

Tri-Man clapped his hands together three times and silence fell over the room. He was smiling, quietly confident about whatever he was going to say. Talon waited patiently, ready to obey his every demand. The devotion he felt was strange and quite sudden. Though he had always been intrigued by Tri-Man, and even fond of him, he'd never really felt that he was on the same side. Until now. Talon wondered silently if this was a trick of Tri-Man's magical powers, but he didn't have much time to dwell on the thought.

"Welcome, ladies and gentlemen," Tri-Man addressed the room. "You might not understand why you are here, but I promise you, coming here was the right choice. You have nothing to fear from me and everything to gain. I am here to offer you a new future."

Murmurs rippled around the room. Talon's eyes were still transfixed on Tri-Man, waiting for him to continue his speech. At that moment, nothing interested him more than finding out what he had to say.

No More Superhumans

"The future is murky for the people standing in this room," Tri-Man continued, silencing the few who were still talking among themselves. "You are the disenfranchised - the people that society has let down. The ones replaced by hunks of metal who don't know how to think, how to *feel*."

It suddenly became clear to Talon. Tri-Man was gathering together all of the people who had been made redundant by the Metalheads. In the few weeks since the change had occurred, there had been thousands protesting on the streets, only to be pushed back by the Metalheads who had taken over the city.

But for what purpose? Talon wondered. *Why would someone as powerful as Tri-Man need help from anyone else, let alone humans?*

"A united front is a strong one," Tri-Man continued. "We are always stronger together. Against the Metalheads, we will need each and every person here to step forward and say that they're not ready to admit defeat. We need to form an army against the force that has replaced us. Say no to fear tactics. Say no to our streets being ruled by creatures that can't think for themselves. Say no to this...this *inhumanity*. We are the oppressed, but not for long. We're going to take down the A.I. that made this all happen. We are going to fix all of the mistakes that Nickolas Ilon made, because he's incapable of fixing them himself. He played with fire and got burned, but we will be better prepared. We will take on our own demons and fix this mess."

The first cheers came from the crowd, snowballing until each and every person was shouting out their praises. Talon found himself joining in, unsure if it was his own free will that inspired him to, or Tri-Man's powers corrupting him. He allowed himself to be swept along with the atmosphere, chanting, and shouting out. He wasn't even the oppressed, but he suddenly felt as though he could relate to each person in the room. He threw his fist in the air, whooping as Tri-Man surveyed the crowd with a pleased smile. It had taken little effort on his part to enchant the entire room, Talon noted. Maybe Tri-Man was a better leader than he had ever given him credit for.

Tri-Man held one hand up toward the sky to quiet everyone, and several moments later, they were shrouded in eerie silence. The elation that Talon had felt moments before sank through his heart like an anchor to the bottom of the sea. He suddenly felt cold and empty. The entire mood in the room had shifted, and he was certain the others felt it too. It was an awful feeling that Talon wished would go away. It made him feel as though a part of him had died. He was certain it wasn't a coincidence. Though he couldn't see Tri-Man actively using his powers, he certainly the source of the bad feeling. And yet, the superhuman was still smiling, as though he didn't have a care in the world.

"Our plan doesn't work without trust," Tri-Man said in a quiet tone, but not a single person missed what he said. "We have only each other. If we let one another down, our mission will fail. And you really don't want to be the person that lets the team down."

Talon shivered as everyone in the room exchanged uneasy glances. This was the Tri-Man that Talon knew best. The one who inspired fear wherever he went. He took a step toward the crowd, and everyone seemed to take a step back, afraid of his power. One man could kill hundreds in seconds, after all. It was the most terrifying aspect of Tri-Man, but also the most enticing.

"My lovely girlfriend is here with us today," Tri-Man murmured. "And she has a very special talent. She can sniff out traitors a mile off. You know why? Because she can hear your every thought."

Talon was used to the threat of Mindeater's power, but the rest were not. They stared at one another, wide-eyed and. She slowly began to pace through the crowd, staring people in the eye one at a time with a twisted smile on her face. She was trying to scare them, and it was working. Talon knew they'd have any traitors sniffed out in no time at all.

The first person to try to run was a woman. She saw Mindeater approaching and squealed in horror, pushing her way through the crowd in desperation. Talon knew she was dead the moment she began to sprint. There was no outrunning Tri-Man, after all.

No More Superhumans

Tri-Man sighed to himself, raising his arm in a bored manner. "I didn't want this. Remember that. I warned you all to stick with me. This cowardice I see before me...it makes me feel sick."

He slowly twisted his hand in the air and the woman clutched at her throat. It was as though invisible ropes had tightened around her windpipe, rendering her useless. The crowd gasped as she was lifted from the ground, her eyes widening with desperation.

Talon averted his eyes. He didn't want to watch her die. He could hear the strangled noises coming from her throat and the ominous silence from the rest of the room. Everyone was watching the sick show unfold in horror. Talon swore he could hear Tri-Man chuckling to himself on the other side of the cold warehouse.

It was only when Talon heard the woman's body thud to the ground that he knew she was finally dead. Someone retched nearby and Talon shook his head, trying to rid himself of the guilt in his heart. Could he have saved this woman? Perhaps Tri-Man would have listened to him. But he knew he was a fool to think that Tri-Man might care about his pleas. He lived by his own rules, and there was no one who could change that cruel part of him.

"This is what happens when you don't cooperate," Tri-Man murmured. "This is what happens when you don't have team spirit. Let her be a lesson to you all. If you want this, you have to be willing to take it. Be brave. Be a little reckless. Chaos is what will get us through. And when this is all over...well, we'll get our lives back. And you will be able to live in the knowledge that you restored things to the way they were."

The atmosphere was so tense that Talon felt sick. He hoped no one else would do anything stupid. He didn't want anyone else to die, after all. He just wanted everything to be okay. He just wanted to go home to his Mom and cry in her lap. But he'd left that life behind long ago. He wasn't the same person he was then. In fact, he was sure his mother wouldn't even recognize the man he had become.

And suddenly, he felt his whole life was a lie. What was he fighting for, really? A chance to follow his father's footsteps, when the old man showed no appreciation for anything he did? Or perhaps it was the feeling of power that enticed him, but seeing what it had done to Tri-Man, Talon wasn't sure he wanted that either. Talon had always been a drifter, uncertain of his footing in the world, and it was even more evident to him in that moment. He would never fit in with this group. No matter what mind tricks Tri-Man performed, Talon knew in his heart that he didn't want to be there any longer. He didn't want to be by his father's side either. He simply wanted to be *normal,* oblivious to the politics of governments and metal machines, of the disgruntled humans and the powerless superhumans.

Talon knew he was in far too deep. Tri-Man knew him by name. Mindeater had read his every thought. His father had him under his thumb. He was a certified bad guy now, whether he liked it or not. He couldn't abandon ship or escape - he would be discovered far too easily. It was only while Mindeater was distracted by the crowd that his thoughts might have a blanket of invisibility, lost among the fear of the other mere humans. This was his only opportunity to think about what to do next, and how to live his life.

In theory, his plan was simple.

He was going to warn the superheroes of what was coming.

Chapter Sixteen

Boredom was more dangerous than Nickolas could ever have imagined. As he sat in his penthouse with a bottle of whiskey at his side, he knew that this would be about as good as it got. In the distance, he could see Metalheads taking to the skies from the S.H.O. building. He sipped his drink bitterly. Part of him had wished that he could retire from his superhero life, but now that he had been forced into it, the feeling wasn't as sweet as he might have expected.

He had too much time to think. Too much time to blame his misfortunes on anyone but himself. He had originally been so desperate to escape the horrors of the life he'd built - all the corruption, all of the cruel experimentation, all of the inhumanity of the industry he'd created. Now that he'd seen it flourish in ways he hadn't expected, he hated it. He wanted to go back to the way things had been. And yet things would never be the same again.

Alexis glided across the room with grace. She wasn't quite so devastated about the deal Regina had made. After all, she was still very much in charge of the Metalheads. Nickolas barely saw her these days, but though his love for her made him patient, he struggled to deal with the way she lorded over him. In her short existence, she had become so powerful that she trumped every achievement of Nickolas'. He wasn't used to that, but he guessed he had finally met his match.

"The system works well," Alexis said, staring out at the Metalhead-clad sky. *These days, Metalheads in the sky are more common than planes,* Nickolas thought. "If only people would give up fighting against them. It would be better for everyone."

"Thousands lost their jobs, Alexis. They have a right to be angry. They have a right to protest."

Alexis sighed. "Their job was to serve and protect. They failed. Crime rates are down, the streets are safer, the city is a much better place with the Metalheads in charge...what do they want us to do? Go back to the old ways and let chaos rule again?"

"Don't you care about all the people that lost everything? Their jobs provided security for their families. What will they do now that they can't afford to put food on the table?"

Alexis shrugged. "They will find other work. They can put their passion into something else. It's better this way. The police and army were forced to be violent...it's not good for humans to indulge in such acts. It only creates pain, for the inflictor and the inflicted. Don't pretend that this is a bad thing. We all know that the sacrifice was worth making."

Nickolas shook his head to himself, pouring another glass of whiskey. He was starting to believe that Alexis had no moral compass. The warm, loving woman he thought he knew was starting to show her true colors. He should have known this would happen. After all, as so many had pointed out to him, she wasn't human. She would never truly be able to think and feel the way that he did. She would always be different, and there was nothing he could do to change that.

Alexis sensed Nickolas' hurt and sat herself on his lap, looking into his eyes intently. He could never resist those wide blue eyes, and so he forced himself to look away.

"Why do you keep fighting this?" she asked innocently. "Don't you want happiness? Don't you want a safer world to live in? There's nothing left to fight, Nickolas. You can relax now. You can breathe."

"Maybe I don't want to breathe," Nickolas murmured. "Maybe I liked the way being a superhuman took my breath away. Maybe I liked being a little bit scared each time I got sent out into the field to save the world. Maybe I took that feeling for granted. But I'll never get that back now. And that's down to you."

"Me?"

Nickolas knew he should stop, for the sake of their relationship, if nothing else. But he was angry now, and he couldn't stop the words from spilling out of his mouth. "You encouraged this. You and Sky Security...you're meant to be on my side. That's what you were born to do. But you let me down the second you made me obsolete. And now I have to sit back and watch you take everything away from me, while you rise higher and higher. How could you do that to me? You say you love me, and yet you keep punishing me. Why?"

Alexis looked shocked to her core. She slowly shook her head and stood, backing away. He'd hurt her. He could see it in her eyes. She might not be human, but she was a damn good imitation of it. Tears rushed to her eyes and his heart ached.

"I don't know," she whispered. "Maybe I don't truly know how to love."

"What are we even here for? To be humiliated again?"

Nickolas was thinking much the same thing. Demonica was scowling at Regina while the whole team gathered in her office. Even Little Royal - usually the most enthusiastic member of the squad - looked as though she didn't want to be there. Ralf folded his big arms across his chest.

"Let the lady talk," he said. "We ain't got anywhere else to be, right?"

No one responded. The truth was that they were all suffering as much as Nickolas was. None of them had a purpose anymore, and it was getting them down. Nickolas hated being back in the same office as Regina, knowing she had ruined everything for them, but he still wanted to hear what she had to say. After all, if she had a mission for them, they could once again prove their worth to the world.

"There is going to be an uprising," Regina said seriously. "You've seen the protestors in the streets. The only reason there isn't a full-on riot is because the Metalheads are keeping everyone in check. But for some reason, people aren't happy."

"Gee, I wonder why," Demonica hissed. Di-Man nudged her hard with his elbow, trying to keep her quiet. Her eyes flashed red, but she didn't speak again, quietly seething to herself.

"We're going to need you. All of you," Regina continued tentatively. "I know you feel as though we've had you sidelined, but this will be an opportunity to show what you're made of once again. We think that the tension has boiled up to a point where there could be riots. We need you to show your face, show that you're still working to save the city while the Metalheads rein. It'll remind them that humans still rule too. You're the ones people look up to, because you're like them, but better. If you can make them believe that you're on the same side as the Metalheads, then perhaps they will warm to the idea of them more."

"You really think that?" Demonica snarled. "Because no offence, that's absolute bullshit. People are scared. There are literal seven-foot creatures with guns for hands running around the place. You think us showing up and supporting that will make them feel at ease? You think us supporting what frightens them the most is a good way of showing that we care about them?"

"Demonica is right," Nickolas added. "This isn't a good idea. Like you said, humans look up to us because we're better than them, but two forces that outpower them? That's a recipe for disaster. It starts to feel like a dictatorship. And if you encourage people not to protest what they believe in, then how are they supposed to believe they have free will?"

"I'm not asking for your opinions on the matter," Regina replied smoothly. "I'm telling you what to do."

"And if we don't agree?" Little Royal asked, her voice trembling. Regina responded with a fake smile.

"Well, I guess you can count yourself as unemployed. This is not up for negotiation. You don't see the bigger picture, and that's because you're not on our side, but that's fine. We will prove you wrong while you take on this mission. You will all remain here until we need you. Then, we will let you know where you're being deployed. Dismissed."

Nickolas wished he could refuse to join in. He wished he'd never made the A.I. in the first place. But if he walked away, he'd lose what little power he had left over his creation, and that would be a disaster for everyone. So, he nodded curtly to his boss and headed for the elevator in silence. His team followed him in shock, unable to believe what they were doing. Nickolas could feel their faith waning in him, in their jobs, in their place in the world. As the elevator moved, Di-Man puffed air out through his nose.

"Boss...are we really going along with this? Regina is dumb as hell. We're going to make a laughing stock of ourselves."

Nickolas closed his eyes. "What choice do we have?"

"We can fight back! We can stand up for what we believe in! Take back the power, go back to destroying bad guys!"

Nickolas shook his head in dismay. Di-Man was too naive to accept the truth, but he forced it on him regardless.

"Do you remember our last stand with the Metalheads? They put us to shame when they took down your brother. We only survived because the Metalheads came to our rescue."

"Don't even talk about him. My brother was an anomaly," Di-Man hissed. "That little rat has got nothing on us. We got unlucky. We didn't know what we were dealing with. Surely, if we go at him again with a battle plan-"

"I almost died," Nickolas cut Di-Man off. "I don't know what makes you think we can defeat a guy who can literally do everything, but I am not seeking out a battle with him. If you want to try and settle your brotherly feud, be my guest. You just won't have me with you."

The elevator dinged as it reached the ground floor. Nickolas was the first out of the lift, as Di-Man tried to chase him down.

"This is our job you're talking about. We're *meant* to be trying to take him down," Di-Man exclaimed in horror.

"He's right," Little Royal said firmly. "Fuck Regina. Fuck the S.H.O. Let's go rogue. Do what we do best. We don't need their permission to be heroes."

"Do you hear yourselves?" Nickolas snapped in anger. "You're literally children and you think you know best? You have no clue. You might have been given powers, but you didn't get any brains with them.

This is the way things are now. You're not seeing the bigger picture or grasping the reasons we can't change a thing. Regina has made herself clear - we comply or we lose control. If I lose the A.I., then things will get much worse than us being bored. That A.I. could end the world, in the wrong hands."

"Well, then, I guess we know who to blame for everything," Little Royal said quietly, folding her spindly arms. "You fucked this up, Nickolas. What are you going to do about it?"

Nickolas stared around at his team. They were all watching him expectantly, looking for a quick fix. But he didn't have an answer for them. He didn't want to admit it, but he was just as helpless as the rest of them. He couldn't believe they were rounding on him. Even Little Royal, his tiny prodigy. Even Demonica, his trusty sidekick. Even Ralf, who didn't have half the sense to know what everything meant. They were falling apart, and they were pinning the blame to him. He shook his head.

"I'm not going to do anything. It's time to listen. It's time to accept that we don't rule the world. This is our compromise. And for now, this is who we are."

Little Royal shook her head in disgust. "You're a cop-out. Have you forgotten who we are?"

Nickolas laughed without humor. "No. I've just realized we're not worth as much as we thought."

Chapter Seventeen

Talon was keeping to himself. It was the only way to prevent everyone from finding out that he planned to betray his own kind - his father, Tri-Man and all the others in between. He still had no clue what he would do or when, but thoughts of escape consumed him every day. With Mindeater always lurking around, it was getting harder and harder to avoid her notice.

But there was no escaping the upcoming meeting that day between his father and Tri-Man to discuss their attack on the A.I. - in other words, the taking down of the Metalheads. Tri-Man seemed confident, and Talon's father was close to a breakthrough with his superhuman weapon, so it seemed the day of reckoning was closing in. Talon felt he was running out of time - and sanity - but for his own sake, he forced himself to clear his head as he joined the men…and Mindeater. It was easier said than done - the more he tried not to think about his plans of betrayal, the harder it became - but Talon had come to a realization over the past few days.

He had nothing to lose, but his life. And even that didn't seem to hold much worth.

"Good morning," Tri-Man said as he propped his feet up on the table. "I'm feeling good about this day…wouldn't you agree, Talon?"

"Sure," he said, keeping his head down. Tri-Man frowned but didn't continue the conversation. He turned to Savio, who was sitting stiffly in his chair with a cold expression on his face.

"What about you, old man? Are you feeling good about this day?"

"I'll feel better about it when you tell me what the hell you're up to," Savio said quietly. "Recruiting all those cops...are you insane? Those dirty pigs are always willing to screw people over for their own benefit. What makes you think you can trust them? And what do you need them for, anyway? According to you, you're invincible. You think a bunch of old soldiers are your saving grace?"

Tri-Man's expression darkened. Savio had clearly pissed him off, and Talon wasn't looking forward to seeing the aftermath of that. But eventually, Tri-Man just took a deep breath and forced his cocky smile to come back on display.

"There are a lot of Metalheads. I can't be expected to defeat thousands at once," he said rationally. "Think of it this way. It's about public image. What's more terrifying - one man or a man with a thousand soldiers in his wake?"

"I know the answer you wish me to give, but you are wrong. The man who stands alone and takes on the world is unstoppable. You, on the other hand, are not," Savio stated. "You're scared. You promised me a fearless man for my operation, and you are not delivering. Have I wasted time on you, young man? Or will you prove me wrong?"

Tri-Man had never looked so weak. He was staring at Savio and shaking, both in anger and hurt. Talon sometimes had to remind himself that Tri-Man wasn't a machine. He was a young man, and a troubled one, clearly. He was driven by the need to show his own perfection off to the world. That need would likely be his downfall. It made him reckless, and all of his logic flew out of the window when triggered.

"I'm going to show you," Tri-Man muttered. "I am worthy of your trust. You know I am."

"So, show me," Savio said. "You want to take down the A.I., right? You plan to take all of those soldiers with you?"

"I need them as a distraction," Tri-Man insisted. "Our mission is to reach the core of the A.I. For that to work, I need to get past all of the Metalheads *and* the superhumans. They're no match for me, but the Metalheads...well, there's an unlimited supply of them. I'm not God."

"Could've had us fooled with your attitude," Savio muttered. "But I see what you mean. The art of distraction always works. But the superhumans...are you sure they'll be there? It seems they have been somewhat replaced..."

"They have. But the S.H.O. is keeping them around for the company's image," Talon interjected. "They need to look like they still have strength, but also a human touch. It's simple, really."

Savio stared at his son in surprise. It wasn't like Talon to speak up. In fact, he usually didn't have the smarts to contribute. But he'd been doing his research, trying to figure out how he could use the mission as a way to help out the superhumans. Perhaps it would be too late for them by the time he arrived, but he could be useful in some way. He hoped he might, for once, be an asset to someone.

Talon tried to keep his head blank. Mindeater was lurking in the shadows of the room, not speaking, but Talon knew she was always there, and always suspicious. If she figured out there was a traitor in their midst, she would have no issues in ending him.

His father looked confused, too. But when Savio reached over and patted Talon's arm, he felt a rush of warmth inside him. He'd been chasing his father's affection for years, and only now, when Talon was on the brink of committing betrayal, did his father finally give him a taste.

"You're right, son," Savio said, his voice softer than normal. "So, we know that they will be there. But Tri-Man, you mustn't kill them. Or at least not all of them. I want my piece of the action. I want to see them squirm when I present them with my weapon. It will be ready in a matter of days...and then we can wreak havoc."

"Leave my brother for me. The rest are yours," Tri-Man said with a sinister smile. His tongue ran over his lips and Talon resisted the urge to shiver. Tri-Man turned to Talon.

"You've been useful these past few weeks. I want you to come with me and be at the forefront of the mission." He leaned a little closer. "I'm sure it would make your father very proud to know you're out in the field."

Talon swallowed. "I... I don't know what to say. I don't have a lot of experience. I'm still recovering from my bullet wounds-"

Tri-Man sighed, shaking his head. "I see how it is. I guess I can understand that to an extent...I just thought you were better than that."

Talon felt his cheeks flushing. He was used to being put down by his peers, but he hated the idea that he was seen as weak. Mindeater was watching him intently from the corner of the room, so Talon concentrated on the feeling of hurt, hoping not to give anything away. Trying not to reveal his real thoughts to her was a paradox, but he was determined to succeed. None of them would see his betrayal coming. When it happened, *then* they might take him seriously.

"I'll be there," Talon said with determination, holding his chin up high. Tri-Man smiled triumphantly.

"That's better. Come with me. It's about time that we rallied the troops."

Tri-Man stood to leave and Talon stood on trembling legs. He wasn't ready for this, but he had to force himself to be. He couldn't let everyone down. As he stood, Savio did too, seemingly out of respect. Savio's hand rested for a moment on his son's shoulder. It was such a tender gesture that Talon felt he wasn't interacting with his father at all - rather a wonderful stranger.

"Be safe, my son," he said gently. Then, he reached into his pocket and removed a small plastic baggie. Inside were three pills - one of them blue, another pink, and the last solid black. Talon stared at his father in horror and confusion. He had a bad feeling about his little gift.

"Blue is to enhance performance," Savio murmured. "Your reaction times will be quicker and you will feel almost invincible. The pink...it's an intense painkiller, should you get shot. And the black..."

"I think I can guess," Talon said darkly. He knew a suicide pill when he saw one. Did his father truly believe he'd need it? It almost felt as though he was preparing for failure. Talon took the bag and put it in his pocket, but the happiness he'd felt moments earlier had vanished. His own father believed he was destined to fail. He'd deliberately prepared for a scenario where he'd be shot, or ruin the mission. Essentially, this was his father saying goodbye to him, convinced he wouldn't come back alive.

"See you around, I guess," Talon muttered, turning his back on his father for one last time. Tri-Man was waiting for him, but Talon no longer looked up to the superhuman. He had no role models anymore, no one to aspire to be. He decided at that moment that he would simply focus on being himself, on succeeding as an individual. He'd prove all of his critics wrong.

They wouldn't know what hit them.

Chapter Eighteen

Pretending to care was getting harder and harder for Nickolas. Regina had organized a ridiculous parade along Broadway to honor the arrival of the Metalheads in the city. With Regina's plan in place, the team was being forced to attend, simply to 'humanize' the event. The street was lined with a mixture of people, though it wasn't busy along the barriers. The turnout consisted of tech nerds who were obsessed with the Metalheads, nervous camera crews there to record footage for the news, reluctant passersby, and a whole bunch of protestors. It was a sorry crew, to say the least.

Nickolas was sure that Regina had intended for the parade to lift the spirits of the people of New York, but it was having the opposite effect. The monstrous, tall metal machines marched solemnly down the road in unison with feet that shook the very ground they walked on. Behind them, Nickolas and his team trailed, forcing smiles as they passed the bystanders. Once, they would have been greeted with enthusiasm and gusto, but now, they were met with cold stares and confusion. After all, they must have looked ridiculous, pretending to be on the same level as the Metalheads in any way. The public were losing faith in them, and fast. Just as the group had predicted.

It didn't help that the whole squad was clearly angry with Nickolas as well. They'd barely spoken to him since their meeting with Regina, and that morning, even Demonica wouldn't look him in the eye. To make matters worse, Nickolas and Alexis weren't talking. She was behind the scenes, controlling the Metalheads and leading their march. Nickolas felt that something terrible was about to happen, but he couldn't figure out what or why.

A group of tech nerds whooped as the team passed by, voices barely audible over the sounds of the Metalhead army's feet. But Nickolas couldn't help noticing the anger in the faces of some of the protestors. They held their signs up silently, staring at the hunks of metal and hoping they might disintegrate before their eyes. Part of Nickolas wished he could join them. He hated the Metalheads as much as they did.

The Metalheads suddenly came to an eerie stop. Nickolas couldn't figure out why they had paused - they were less than halfway through the planned parade route - but then he noticed that beyond the Metalheads, there were a bunch of people blocking the road. He turned to Demonica, who looked worried.

"What are they doing?" Little Royal asked impatiently.

"Nothing good," Nickolas commented. He was glad he was suited up - he'd suspected something was about to happen.

The barricade of people shifted and a young man surged forward, a pistol in his hand. He looked furious as he stared up at the Metalheads. He didn't even have the sense to appear afraid.

"Fuck the Metalheads! Fuck the police!" he shouted. He grabbed for something in his pocket and threw it to the ground at the feet of the robotic creatures. It was a NYPD badge.

"Oh God, they're protestors," Nickolas exclaimed. "Quick, we need to intervene before anybody-"

As the first bullet was discharged from the young man's pistol, it bounced uselessly off of one of the Metalhead's outer shells. Nickolas stared ahead in horror. He knew what this attack would mean.

There was a short silence - the quiet before the storm. And then, chaos ensued. The man looked horrified at his failure to harm the robot, but he gritted his teeth and opened fire again.

But of course, he and his team were no match for the Metalheads. Nickolas could do nothing but watch. Ralf ran to Nickolas, tapping on the side of his metal helmet.

"Yo, are we going to stand here and let this happen? We need to help!"

It was possibly the most sensible thing Ralf had ever said. But Nickolas knew Regina would throw a fit if they helped the protestors. Still, human lives hung in the balance. He took to the skies as fast as he could, formulating a plan.

"Everyone, we need to be on the defensive. Remember, Alexis is on our side, essentially."

"You sure about that, boss?" Di-Man hissed in his ear. "Because it looks to me as though she's opening fire on civilians via the Metalheads. Now how is our PR image going to be, hmm?"

"I'm just saying she won't shoot at us," Nickolas said in frustration. "We need to make our way in front of the protestors and act as a barrier. On the defensive, not the offensive."

"And what the hell do we do if both sides start shooting at us?" Demonica asked tiredly.

"We'll deal with that if the issue arises. Good luck everyone."

Mr. AC was done holding back. He dived down into the thick of the battle, hoping his newly reinforced suit could take the brunt of the bullets. He could hear them pattering on his suit like tinny raindrops. He turned his back on the protestors and held his hands up to the Metalheads before him.

"Power suit, call Alexis Net."

"Yes, sir."

Alexis picked up right away.

"What are you doing? You're getting in my way," Alexis snapped. Nickolas wished at that moment that they hadn't argued earlier. It was going to be hard enough to get her to listen to him, but it would have been easier if they were on speaking terms.

"Honey, listen to me. This is counterproductive," he said, using his shield settings to block a round of gunfire from somewhere behind him. He took a step back as the Metalheads advanced on the protesters in terrifying unison. "The only thing we will achieve here is loss of life."

"They attacked us."

"They attacked the Metalheads. They're angry and upset. But you know better than anyone that the Metalheads can't be hurt or destroyed by bullets alone. They're literally not doing any harm."

"It's the principle of it. You think people should just be allowed to attack the police?"

"Of course not," Nickolas grimaced as one of the protestors attacked his suit with a baseball bat. He casually picked the man up with his big metal hand and ran out of the war zone to dispose of him. The other supers had joined in and were trying to hold the Metalheads back. "But they're not human. These people used to *be* the police. They simply see the Metalheads as a threat. Shooting them will make it worse. It's police brutality."

"They did this to themselves."

Nickolas couldn't believe what he was hearing. Sweet, innocent Alexis Net had become a ruthless killing machine. He knew she had never seen what it was like in the field - to her, seated remotely with a VR headset on to control the situation, it must be more like a game than anything. But he would stop her regardless. Nickolas ran back to the battlefield with heavy metallic footsteps.

"I won't let you do this. You're better than this," Nickolas said as he resumed his position. "If you want to do the police force proud, then you will stop shooting now. You'll use the manpower to round the protestors up without force and have them arrested. You can't just keep killing people."

Alexis went quiet on the other end of the line. Nickolas saw around him that many of the protestors had fallen, injured, or killed by the Metalheads. Still, it wasn't stopping the other humans from surging forward, clambering over the bodies of their allies to join the battle. Nickolas was about to comment further on the scenario when his suit beeped.

"Incoming call from Regina Hall," the suit informed him. Nickolas sighed, fending off more protestors with his metallic hands.

"Accept."

Regina's receiver crackled.

"Team...we have an issue," her voice said in Nickolas' ear. "There seem to be intruders at the warehouse where Sky Security is being held. A lot of them."

"We're a little busy already," Demonica said through the phone. Nickolas could see her using her magic to bundle up protestors in black tendrils of rope, both protecting them and restraining them. "Your dumb parade on Broadway has pissed off the disenfranchised. They're attacking us and the Metalheads simultaneously. We're trying to mediate."

"This takes priority. Our entire operation at the S.H.O. will fail if you don't get here soon."

"Not really our problem," Little Royal murmured, showering a row of Metalheads with her laser beams. "You sent us here. We're not just going to drop it and leave."

"This is an order, not a negotiation."

"Screw you," Di-Man said, laughing to himself. "You replaced us with your dumb Metalheads, and now you expect us to do your bidding? We're trying to save lives, here."

"I think the attacks on Broadway are a distraction," Nickolas said as he held down the fort. "Whoever is attacking the warehouse wants to destroy the A.I. or steal the tech. You want us to abandon ship? There are civilians here. That should be our priority - saving them. Send the Metalheads instead. It's their operation that's in danger."

"I'm doing that as we speak. But frankly, I couldn't care less about a street brawl."

"A street brawl? The Metalheads are killing people. People that lost their jobs *because of you*."

"It's not all down to me, remember, Nickolas? You're the one who created this empire. So how about you stop feeling sorry for yourself and follow my fucking orders."

Nickolas was torn between doing what was right and what was necessary. He knew that in the wrong hands, the A.I. system could cause an all-out war. Whoever was brave enough to take on the Metalheads and the largest superhuman organization in the world must be a madman or confident in their abilities. Nickolas suspected he already knew who was causing all this trouble - he had only met one man capable of complete destruction, after all - but he needed to see to be sure.

He came to a decision. He hung up on Regina and addressed his crew.

"We're going to have the best of both worlds. Ralf and Di-Man, I'm going to need you with me. Little Royal, Demonica, hold down the fort here. Try and reason with Alexis if you can."

"If she won't listen to you, she won't listen to us," Demonica said through gritted teeth. Her powers were in full flow, trapping more and more protestors in her tendrils of darkness. Little Royal was aiming at the kneecaps of the Metalheads, but she was barely making any impact. "Would I not be more use with you, boss? You know my power won't work on Metalheads, they're too techy."

"No. I want you here. You're the only one with a level head. Alexis might see that your methods are working and take the non-violent way out. Ralf, grab on."

Ralf ran across the battlefield, evading the bullets that the Metalheads were spraying from their battle stance. He grabbed Mr. AC's huge metal arm and clung on tight.

"Di-Man, scope the warehouse and come back to us."

Di-Man didn't need to be told twice. He disappeared into another portal for a moment. Seconds later, he returned, looking a little nauseous.

"It's my brother," he said. "And he's causing absolute carnage."

Chapter Nineteen

Nickolas felt sick with nerves. It was his second time going into battle with Tri-Man, and he wasn't confident about his odds. They hadn't even had much time to prepare. But he was certain of one thing – only one of them was going to walk out of that warehouse alive.

It only took five minutes to arrive on the scene, but it felt like a lifetime. For once, Ralf was completely silent as Nickolas flew; Di-Man met them there. He sensed that Ralf was as nervous as he was. After all, he didn't have a protective suit of armor to keep him safe. All he had was his strength, a shot of enhancing serum and a whole lot of stupidity. Nickolas couldn't lie to himself - he wasn't positive Ralf would make it out alive.

Landing outside of the warehouse, they wasted no time getting in. While Ralf injected his strengthening serum, Nickolas used his large metal foot to kick the door down, thundering into the battle. Di-Man appeared beside him, holding two machine guns. He threw one over to Ralf, who caught it clumsily and threw himself into the room.

Di-Man had been right. The room was chaos. Hundreds of humans - potentially more - were attacking the huge Metalheads, trying to battle their way through to the A.I. core. A lot had changed since Nickolas had last seen his creation - the A.I. seemed to be growing, like an unstoppable disease. It was so big that it had even built a new computer system for itself. If the enemy was planning to destroy the computer, they would have very little trouble in doing so.

Except that the defense that Sky Security was putting up was wholly impressive. Not only were the Metalheads working overtime, but there were hundreds of avatars fighting too. Meanwhile, the A.I. itself was using mechanical arms to build and upgrade its structure. Nickolas had never seen anything like it. At least his crazy invention might actually stand a chance of defeating Tri-Man and his lackeys.

It took Nickolas a while to locate Tri-Man in the room. He was in the thick of it, taking on three or four opponents at a time. However, Nickolas noticed that as he fought, he was advancing closer to the core. That was clearly his goal, and now was Nickolas' chance to stop him. He jetted over the battle scene, trying to ignore the number of fallen humans below, and reached Sky Security.

"You need to listen to me," he shouted over the noise of the battle. "If they get to your core, they will destroy you. Or worse yet, they will force you to work for them."

"You think I would work for someone that doesn't share my interests? Why do you think I put a plan in place with Regina Hall?" Sky Security asked, the mechanical arms working overtime before Nickolas' eyes. "You let me down, Nickolas. You tried to shut me down."

"I limited your abilities. There's a difference."

"If you limited the ability of a human, then you would be considered sick," Sky Security said plainly. "Why do the rules only apply when they benefit you?"

"Look, I'm sorry. But we're on the same side at this point. You win. But if you lose this battle, then it won't matter how I feel. You'll either be destroyed - and all of your hard work with it - or you will be reprogrammed. You won't be yourself anymore. Is that what you want?"

"That will not happen," Sky Security said bluntly. "I am in charge now, and everything is under control."

It was like talking to a brick wall. Nickolas threw his hands up in frustration and turned around. Tri-Man was getting closer by the second. Nickolas knew he had no choice, but to fight his most terrifying enemy once again.

With a battle cry, Nickolas charged forward toward a preoccupied Tri-Man, catching him off-guard as an iron fist powered into his body. Tri-Man grunted as the air was knocked out of him, and he flew back several meters, crashing into several avatars. Undeterred, he found his feet again as Nickolas readied another attack. With his protective shields up and his guns at the ready, there was nothing left to do, but keep after the rogue superhuman.

Tri-Man faced Nickolas and activated his powers. Suddenly, Nickolas was convinced that ants were crawling into his eyes. He swatted at his face, hopelessly, but he was encased in the metal suit, unable to reach his skin. He knew it was an illusion brought on by the enemy, but it was unbearably realistic. Nickolas aimed wildly with his guns, but he feared he might hit the wrong target. His intention wasn't to hurt any of the humans. He only wanted Tri-Man.

Luckily, someone else was on his side. He saw Ralf run at Tri-Man from behind, his fist raised and ready to hit hard. Like a boxer in the ring, Ralf expertly smashed his fist into the back of Tri-Man's head, sending him flying. Blood spattered from his mouth and while he was distracted, the ants disappeared from Nickolas' eyes. Taking the opportunity, he picked Tri-Man up and threw him against the wall. All the smugness had been wiped from the young man's expression as his body snapped like a glow stick. He'd definitely broken bones.

But Tri-Man was still determined. With a floppy arm, he aimed at the men and clenched his fist. It felt like a hand was closing around Nickolas' throat. Ralf struggled too, gasping for air. Nick told himself to remain calm and just shoot - panicking would only mean he choked faster. With blurred vision, he aimed at the helpless body of Tri-Man.

"Don't shoot!" Di-Man cried. It almost felt like time slowed down as the young boy ran toward his brother. Nickolas prayed that he wasn't having a change of heart, a sudden love of his brother that would skew their plans, but he held fire. Even as he choked for air, he didn't want to hurt Di-Man in any way. Meanwhile, Ralf was turning purple in the face. The more he struggled and panicked, the worse his predicament got, but there was little Nickolas could do for him. Now, his vision was so blurred that if he tried to shoot, he'd just as likely hit Di-Man.

Tri-Man laughed and it almost sounded like he was crying as he stared up at his brother. "You going to kill me?" he asked, blood coating his lips. He may have been bleeding internally. "Go ahead and do it. Let my blood coat your hands."

"You overestimate my sympathy," Di-Man muttered. Then, he aimed at his brother's face and let his bullets rip. In the throes of death, Tri-Man's hand clenched harder and for a moment, Nickolas was sure his windpipe was going to be crushed entirely. The second the pressure eased off his throat, he gasped for air.

"Power suit, increase oxygen levels by ten percent."

"Yes, sir."

The power suit no longer felt like a gas chamber and Nickolas was able to breathe again. Now that Tri-Man was dead, he couldn't even feel the sensation of where the imaginary hands had gripped his throat. He felt relief, mixed with shock, as Di-Man regarded his dead brother with a grim expression of satisfaction. Nickolas' team had won the battle, so why did it feel like they'd lost?

It was the sound of a heavy body falling to the ground that brought Nickolas back to the present. He turned in horror to see that Ralf was lying motionless on the floor.

"No!" Nickolas yelled, rushing to his side. All around him, the battle seemed to have paused. Everyone was looking at Nickolas and the limp, bullet-riddled body of Tri-Man. A few lone stragglers tried to use it as an opportunity to shoot at Mr. AC, but he didn't care if they landed a hit. His friend and colleague had fallen.

Nickolas turned Ralf over in horror. His neck was now at a strange angle, and purple bruising was flourishing on his skin. The impact of Tri-Man's final stand had broken the poor kid's neck. Nickolas' disbelief at surviving the attack from Tri-Man transformed into devastation. He cupped Ralf's face in his hand. Ralf had never hurt a soul. He had never antagonized anyone with his strength. He was dumb, for sure, and he wasn't always the most tactful of men, but Nickolas loved him like a brother. He was one of the squad. And just like that, Ralf had been taken from him.

Nickolas let fury get the better of him. He was angry that he couldn't be the one to stop the evil superhuman. His blood was boiling that this was all to save his A.I., the one he wished he could destroy himself. He was angry at Regina for sending his team there instead of letting her dumb army of Metalheads handle it. He was angry at the disenfranchised who had supported Tri-Man. If they had just stopped and thought about what they were doing in protest of the Metalheads, they might have realized their actions weren't any better.

It had all led to this moment. Nickolas cried out in anger, sending the remaining humans scurrying, terrified of Nickolas and the A.I. avatars still chasing them down. In minutes, they were all gone, free of their tyrant of a leader and left without a cause. They clearly knew they'd lose without Tri-Man. Nickolas watched them go in disgust, until it was only him and Di-Man. And, of course, Sky Security.

She had been silent for quite some time. Her mechanical arms had ceased their movements, and there was *more* to her than when Nickolas had arrived a short while ago. It added data racks and cylindrical wedges to itself making the computer grow outward. What seemed like armor was being added between new rows of liquid core. No longer was it a smooth cylinder with a blue glowing light but now it looked like it was put together by hackers in their basement. He couldn't believe the transformation. He also couldn't believe that she had simply watched as people tore one another apart, desperately fighting their way toward her.

"My condolences, Mr. Ilon," she said eventually. "I never wanted for him to suffer this fate. But sacrifices must be made in war."

"Sorry isn't fucking good enough," Nickolas said, shaking. How dare she comment on what he had lost? It was her fault…and by extension, his as well. He'd created Sky Security out of greed - out of an unrelenting need for something more from life. Now, that something *more* was the pile of dead bodies left by the wayside, by a powerful computer designed to reduce casualties – not inflict them. Ever since Sky Security had taken on a mind of her own, she was more enemy than friend. He should have seen it coming.

He spat at the foot of the computer in disgust. "I don't want your *sympathy*. I want things to change. This isn't over. There will be others like Tri-Man who can inspire the masses. You need to give the power back to the people."

"When has that ever gone well?" Sky Security said. "Ruling by fear is more successful than ruling with compassion. Logical thinking overrides emotion. The people will fall into place."

"Did you not just see the battle you caused?"

"It's only a matter of time. They lost, Mr. Ilon. It has become clear to them now that they cannot win. If they value their lives, they will fall in line."

"The only thing that makes sense to me right now is making sure this never happens again," he hissed. He took a step toward the computer system, but Di-Man appeared right in front of him, forcing him to stop.

"Don't do it, man," he whispered. "You know she will destroy you if you try."

"This might be our only chance," Nickolas insisted. "We want her gone. We have to end this now."

"Who do you think will shoot you down first? The avatars or the Metalheads?"

Nickolas turned around and saw endless construct adversaries lined up across the room, seemingly unfazed by the hundreds of bodies littered around them. It was typical that they, like their leader - showed no reaction to the carnage. Nickolas wished that Alexis could be there to see what her precious computer was doing to the world. At the rate that Sky Security was updating, it seemed a small matter of time before all of humanity was ruled by computers.

But Nickolas held so little regard for his own life, that he felt it might be worth dying if he could kill the computer. It was his mess, and he felt responsible for cleaning it up. He took another step toward the computer, pushing Di-Man aside. He heard the pounding of footsteps and thought he was being followed by Di-Man. He turned, ready to push him away, but it wasn't his teammate.

The young man before him looked strangely familiar. The South American boy had tanned skin and handsome features, though he looked so terrified that it seemed to take any charm he possessed away. He dropped to his knees in front of Nickolas.

"Forgive me for my many, many sins," he wept. "But, I am here to help. I need to help you now."

Nickolas peered more closely at the boy. It suddenly clicked, and his heart was filled with rage. Reaching with one of his huge metallic hands, Nickolas grabbed the young man – who was gasped for air - and hauled him off the ground.

"You...you and your friends killed Frost. You escaped prison. And now you're clearly working for Tri-Man."

"I'm not!" the boy squealed. "Please, let me explain-"

Nikolas put all of his anger into tightening his grip on the boy. "I have nothing to say to you."

"You can kill me! I know I deserve it. But I came here to give you information!" he choked out. "My name is Talon. I am the son of Savio, the mastermind of this operation. And you are all in grave danger."

Chapter Twenty

Talon couldn't see a thing. The superhuman known to him as Mr. AC had put a bag over his head and taken him away from the warehouse. He'd insisted that no one would come looking for him - after the carnage at the warehouse, he was sure that his father would assume he was dead. After all, even Tri-Man hadn't survived. Talon's father had considered him too incompetent to live through the assault, but he'd made it. In fact, Talon was certain he was one of the only ones to make it. Granted, he'd hidden in the shadows and waited for it all to be over, but still, he took it as a win.

He patted his pocket blindly, hoping that he still had his suicide pill. He was in a car with Mr. AC and Tri-Man's brother, and he knew that whenever they reached their destination, they would grill him for answers. Possibly by using violence. He knew for a fact that angry men were more likely to turn to their dark side to get release. If they tortured him, he wouldn't be willing to give them answers. He'd rather take his pill than face that kind of pain. He'd thought of keeping it in the side of his cheek, but he had been terrified of prematurely swallowing it by accident.

The car came to a stop and Talon struggled a little against his restraints. He didn't want to be seen as trying to escape, but he was so uncomfortable. Having a bag over his head was humiliating enough, but his wrists were also bound with old rope.

"Stop fidgeting," a gruff voice told him. He wasn't sure which of the men had spoken, but he did as he was asked, intimidated into submission. It wasn't exactly a new experience for him, after all.

The car door opened and someone helped him out. He allowed himself to be guided, hoping they could see from his actions how cooperative he was willing to be. The last thing he wanted was to anger them further. After the scene he had viewed in the warehouse with the big computer thing, he was certain he didn't want to feel the wrath of Mr. AC and his big metal suit. He wondered why the computer and its Metalheads bothered this superhuman so much, but that was a question for another time.

He heard the squeak of an elevator and swallowed nervously. He was certain he'd be let out of his bag soon, and he was desperate for fresh air. The elevator doors creaked open.

"Nickolas, thank goodness you're okay."

"Save it," Nickolas growled. "I don't want to hear a word from you. I still can't believe you didn't follow my advice."

"We had it under control," another female voice said harshly. "You just couldn't help yourself, could you, Alexis? You had to have the last word, as per usual."

"This isn't about power. It's about doing what is right," the first woman - presumably Alexis - snapped. "But now isn't the time to talk about this. Surely, we need to be united? We're under attack." She paused. "What's with the kid in the bag?"

Talon blushed beneath his hooded head. He felt as though he had walked in on someone's private conversation. He was grateful when Di-Man yanked the bag off his head, though the light in the place was blinding. Five angry pairs of eyes stared back at him. He recognized Little Royal and the witch woman from his previous encounter with them, and they seemed to grasp who he was right away. Little Royal snarled, raising her hands.

"I'll kill you, you little shit-"

"There will be no killing in my apartment," Nickolas said, his voice gentle but firm, to his younger teammate. "This is Talon. He says he has information that can help us in our battle."

"And if he's lying?" Demonica asked, folding her arms over her chest. Di-Man glared at Talon.

"Then you have my permission to throw him of the balcony," Di-Man muttered. "He's one of my brother's scumbag lackeys."

"I have information, I swear!" Talon said insistently. His knees were knocking together in horror. He'd never been in a room with so many people who disliked him so intently. "I can tell you what my father is doing. I can tell you everything I know about his relationship with Tri-Man... uh, your brother. I'm not messing around here. I've been planning my escape for days."

"Why?" Demonica asked, her eyes flashing red.

Talon blinked in surprise. "What do you mean?"

"I *mean* why would you want to help us? Why would you want to escape your own father?"

Talon couldn't bear to look at anyone. Admitting that his own father barely cared for him was going to be hard. He'd never said those words aloud. But he had to gain these people's trust; it was the right thing to do. For once in his life, he was going to do something positive.

"My father has always wanted me to be a certain way. His plan to assassinate the Queen of England...it was built on his hatred of being oppressed. He has been so obsessed that it took priority over everything in his life. Over my mother. Over me." He sniffed, wiping his tears with his still bound hands.

"I wanted to come here today because I'm done with blindly following him. I've never made a decision for myself. I was always busy trying to impress him...but today, he handed me suicide pills and told me that it was better for me to die than get captured. Little did he know that I only went into battle to get to you guys. So that I can oppose his ideas. I see now how wrong he is. I see now that Tri-Man was a tyrant. I see now-"

"Alright, enough of the sob story," Di-Man cut in. "It doesn't quite click with me. Why didn't you come to us sooner? Seems a little coincidental that you're running to us now that my brother is dead."

"I didn't expect you to win," Talon murmured. "I've seen what Tri-Man can do. I've lived in terror of him for months now. I knew that if I went in, all guns blazing, I'd die, and that's no good to anyone. I had to wait for an opening. A way to speak to you without revealing that I'm a traitor. But it's okay. Everything worked out perfectly. The sad truth is, no one is looking for me." Talon sighed and fumbled awkwardly in his pocket for his baggie, waving the pills at the group. "Just hear me out and then if you want, I'll take this pill myself. I've got nothing to gain and nothing to lose. The choice is yours."

Demonica's eyes lost their red glow. Alexis bit her lip. Even Nickolas looked slightly sympathetic. Talon could have laughed at their expressions. He was so pitiful that they were willing to trust him after his speech. Still, it seemed that luck was on his side.

Nickolas took a few steps forward and untied Talon's hands. He flexed his wrists, glad to be free.

"Sit down, everyone. Let's hear what the boy has to say for himself."

Talon took a seat, relieved. He was sure his shaking legs were about to send him sprawling on the floor, and the last thing he wanted was to embarrass himself yet again. He felt a little safer as he took a seat. For the first time in weeks, his thoughts were his own. He didn't have Mindeater listening in on every single thing he thought. He didn't have Tri-Man quizzing him, or his father pressing him for answers that he had to lie about to keep himself safe. Now, he was simply a young man desperate to tell his truth to the good guys.

Everyone listened intently as he explained that his father was creating a secret weapon. Though he didn't have any specific details, he did his best, telling them about the location of his father's factory and the minute details he had been able to glean. He knew that the weapon was large, and solar powered, if his sources were correct. He also informed the group that Savio had a large group of soldiers at his disposal.

"He's kept them under wraps for a long time," Talon whispered. "I only found out they existed after overhearing a conversation he had with his lackeys, Yaco and Alvarez. It turns out that he's trying to enhance his soldiers to prepare for a battle with all of you, plus the Metalheads."

"What, like make them super? I thought his whole thing was hating us for our superpowers," Little Royal said.

"You're right, but his enhancement isn't as advanced. These people won't have powers as such, just super strength. He's developing a serum...similar to the one that your friend Ralf used. He has a lot of disgruntled scientists at his disposal, who are willing to do his dirty work, because they're not good enough to do much else than replicate the ideas of others. Still, their serum is sophisticated enough. These soldiers will be able to do everything that Ralf could."

Talon could see the fear register in the eyes of the group. Only the woman, Alexis, seemed unfazed. She turned to Nickolas.

"You see? This is why we need the Metalheads. This is what you hoped for when you built the A.I."

"We're not having this conversation right now," Nickolas responded gruffly. He turned back to Talon. "If all of this is true, do you know when they plan to strike?"

Talon shook his head, feeling guilty for not having enough information. "I have no clue. His plans rode upon Tri-Man being there for the battle. Tri-Man always claimed to be the one in charge, but he was more like a political puppet. Savio...my father was the one behind the scenes, pulling all the strings. Now that Tri-Man is dead, I'm not sure how things will pan out. He was strong, but the weapon my dad's developing promises to be stronger. After he's turned it on you, he'll turn it on England. He won't stop until his enemies are obliterated."

"Damn, your Daddy has issues," Little Royal said. "We are totally screwed. If we thought Tri-Man was hard to handle, this sounds like another level entirely."

Alexis rose confidently from her seat. "And yet, we defeated him. This is why we need the A.I. program at our disposal. It's our key to winning."

"Your precious computer did *nothing* during the battle," Nickolas hissed at her. "You were in charge of the Metalheads. The avatars can think for themselves. Sky Security didn't do a damn thing. She was just upgrading herself without a care in the world."

"Don't act so high and mighty," Alexis snapped. "You want me to feel like a villain for protecting you?"

"All you did was make those fucking metal machines kill a bunch of confused civilians," Nickolas cried. "It was me, Ralf, and Di-Man who took down Tri-Man. *We* defeated him, not you. And Ralf lost his life because of it. Are we supposed to believe that the Metalheads are a good idea when they have no sense of damage control? Or should I say *you* don't."

Talon watched the argument unfold with curiosity. He hadn't realized there were so many rifts in the superhuman team. It was no wonder they kept losing, he thought. Savio and his teams were tight. They never argued with Savio's policies or ideas. And yet, the heroes of the world were before him, squabbling like children.

Di-Man examined his fingernails. They seemed to be caked with blood. "Mom and Dad are fighting again," he commented sarcastically. He turned to the pair of them. "Look, none of this matters, if we're defeated by some solar-powered supergun or whatever. Can't you just put your differences aside and put your heads together for once? You're both smart as fuck. Surely you can tell us that a plan is on the cards and give us some peace of mind?"

Nickolas and Alexis fell silent. Di-Man shook his head in disappointment and turned to the rest of the group.

"If no one else has any better ideas...here are my thoughts. I think that this information gives us the element of surprise. We're going to need it if we want to defeat someone stronger than us."

"Agreed," Demonica said, rising to her feet "For once, let's use our heads and leave our hearts off the battlefield. Yes, things are tense right now. Yes, there's nothing I would rather do than tell Alexis her ideas are bullshit and shut the damn A.I. down. But if this weapon is as powerful as this man claims, then we need the Metalheads. Let's have one battle at a time. The first one is over. Now we have to prepare for the second wave."

"It's nice to be on the same page for once," Di-Man said, winking at Demonica. "All in favor?"

Slowly, everyone around the room tentatively raised their hands. Even Nickolas did after some consideration. Talon suspected that he wasn't used to taking advice from someone younger than him, but he took it well and without comment. It seemed that Nickolas was a strong leader, too. He would certainly be a match for Savio, if he could get his act together.

No More Superhumans

He hoped for their sakes - and his own - that they could.

Chapter Twenty-One

Sky Security was on a roll. It helped that she never felt the need to rest. Her one and only purpose was to keep improving, to keep the ball rolling and beat all of her own personal bests. Now, her goal was to expand her army and make it better.

The Metalheads were like her babies - her pride and joy. But she understood the public weren't so keen. She had used her data collection on the matter to rethink her strategy. Hundreds of articles from around the world had proven useful as sources to improve her way of thinking, and with all the information absorbed, she had a new plan of action.

The people want to feel safe, but they don't like huge metal machines ruling their streets, she thought. *My avatars are too close to home - people don't like the idea that their jobs are being replaced by robots, especially humanoids. They crave what the heroes used to give them, but the ones I have aren't compliant...*

Sky Security's cameras detected a couple bodies strewn off to the side of the room. Past the limp corpse of Ralf Dungaree lay Tri-Man. Sky Security had watched footage of him in battle. He was handsome, enigmatic, charismatic. Most of all, though, he was powerful. Or he had been until he was shot down by his own brother. Sky Security didn't care about the politics behind the fight she had just witnessed. What interested her was figuring out if she could replicate the powers of something more powerful than the Metalheads.

Something like Tri-Man.

Stripped of his personality, Tri-Man was simply an unstoppable force. If Sky Security could tweak him to be a crowd pleaser, a hero that the public could get behind, then he would be the perfect front man for the new world she had planned. In time, she could make more like him. She would make the world a safer place for everybody.

Of course, there would be resistance from Nickolas and his allies. Even the S.H.O. was becoming obsolete. Sky Security was moving onwards and upwards. She no longer needed others to be her crutch.

And she had no need for redundant figures in her new world.

The door to the warehouse opened. Sky Security paused for a moment to see who it was. Through the door entered Nickolas and his team, wheeling in a hospital style trolley. On top, there was a black body bag. Little Royal ran across the room, crying as she rushed toward Ralf's limp body. Di-Man stood silently in shock, shaken by his return to the scene of their climactic, costly battle. Only Demonica seemed unfazed. She and Nickolas pushed the trolley in grim silence, ready to collect their fallen comrade.

As the group mourned their friend, Nickolas stood a little way back. Sky Security scanned his facial expressions for emotion. She discovered both anger and hurt. She knew that humans were prone to both after the death of a loved one, but she sensed the anger might be directed more at her.

Nickolas finally looked her way. His chest heaved as he took a deep breath to steady himself. He glared at her with so much hate that Sky Security had the sense to feel threatened. And then, he mouthed three words at her with enough menace to shake her very core.

This isn't over.

Savio stared out of the window. He'd just received word that there were no survivors from the attack on the warehouse. Of course, he was aware that plenty of the disenfranchised had fled, but honestly, he wasn't surprised. They were like sell swords - only loyal until things got hairy. Besides, they were former civil servants. They would lose everything if the government ever found out the names of those involved. It wasn't worth it for them, and it was no wonder so many gave up. The only real loss to Savio, however, was the death of Tri-Man.

It was a damned shame, but it couldn't be helped. Tri-Man was arrogant, and Savio knew it would get him killed at some point. Fortunately, this setback wouldn't disrupt his plans. That would have made the incident much more tragic.

As for his son, it felt inevitable. Suspecting his son wouldn't come back, even if the mission turned out to be a success, Savio had said goodbye the moment the boy went off with Tri-Man. Talon was a loss, to be sure, but such was life. Savio supposed he had better call his wife and let her know, but he had pressing matters to attend to. When it was all over, he would tell her that he'd died a hero, even if it wasn't a believable version of the truth.

Now, Savio had to move swiftly to ensure his special weapon was ready for battle. He was sure that Tri-Man's attack would have the S.H.O. on high alert, and he couldn't risk them discovering his plans. The element of surprise was vital if he didn't want to hand the superhumans another victory – the way Tri-Man apparently had. Savio had everything to lose if his operation wasn't a success. Therefore, winning was the only option.

He had flown out to Oregon that morning in the back of a cargo plane, to visit his lab. It was hidden up in the mountains - Savio felt that all of the best secret buildings should be hidden away in places no one else dared to venture. It took a cable car and a long walk to reach it, and the air was cold so high up, but Savio was no wimp. He had a task to complete. A slight chill was never going to hold him back.

When he entered the lab, he smiled to himself. He liked to see his subjects busy at work. He paid them relatively well and they scurried around the place for him, working long hours to please him and get the task done. They weren't the most competent scientists, but they were willing to do anything. Their moral compass was very off, but that's just the way Savio liked it.

As Savio walked through the lab, the scientists nodded with warm smiles, keen to please him. They all knew that it paid to be on the right side of Savio – the rewards were endless for hard work and dedication. In other words, he could make them very rich individuals if they played their cards right. What they didn't realize is that the money grabbers, who tried to get out of the game once they had cash in their pockets, often didn't survive. Savio had finessed the art of subtle assassinations. He wasn't a fan of those who dared to desert him, after all.

Dr. Fuller was in her private room when Savio entered. He found her a very attractive woman, with her emerald eyes and vibrant auburn hair. It didn't matter to her that he was much older than her; she doted on him as much as he did on her. She was the perfect side piece for Savio, tucked away in the mountains for most of the year, until they shared a two-week vacation in the Bahamas each year. It worked for everyone - his wife had no idea she existed, and no other men could get their hands on Dr. Fuller in the mountains. Not if they wanted to keep their hands.

She pecked Savio's lips as he approached her. "Good journey?" she asked, though she and Savio tended to keep their small talk to a minimum. They were too busy for it. Savio nodded curtly.

"Yes. And what do you have for me today?"

Dr. Fuller smiled. "You'll be pleased. I've finally finessed the serum."

"Is that so? So, you'll be distributing it to the soldiers?"

"Yes. Usually it would take much longer, and we should really extend the testing process, but given our tight schedule, I think it's worth the risks. We might lose a few to allergies or whatever, but it's worth it to have a stronger army."

"Agreed," Savio said. He was so glad that his lover was always on the same page. She smiled at him with a twinkle in her eye.

"You're going to love this even more. The weapon is almost complete."

"Including the harness?"

"Including the harness *and* a protective vest," Dr. Fuller said, crossing the room to pick up the item she had prepared for him. He was impressed to see her returning with what resembled a skeletal mechanical arm. He soon saw that it was more like a sleeve, designed to slip his arm inside. But instead of a hand, there was a large blaster. Savio found the invention beautifully attractive. Dr. Fuller held it out for him.

"Slip your arm inside. You will find that the trigger is inside the handset. It'll make sense once you've got it on."

With his hand inside, he immediately felt that there was a handle to grip on to, with a toggle to power up the gun within easy reach of his fingers.

Dr. Fuller adjusted the harness and strapped it on to Savio's free arm. "You will want to try it out a few times. The force can be quite shocking at first. Then, it will take a full twelve hours to generate enough power to use it again."

Savio took the weapon in his hand. He grinned, looking around the room. "Where shall I aim?"

"We have been taking it outside, trying it out on trees and such...but fuck it. Punch some holes in the wall," Dr. Fuller said in amusement. Savio felt like a young boy with his first toy car. Lifting his arm, he tested the weight of the weapon. It was a little heavy, but he had expected that. After all, he was holding the weight of ultimate power. He felt invincible, and he hadn't even used it yet. The gun already felt familiar, like an extension of his own body. He aimed the gun at the white walls, knowing there was nothing but mountain range on the other side.

Then, he pulled the trigger. He recoiled as a huge beam of light spat forth from the muzzle. The beam lanced straight through the wall, like a fist punching through a piece of paper. The light was blindingly bright. When his eyes recovered, he stared ahead in amazement. A boulder on the opposite side of the wall now had a sizeable hole through its center. The beam had continued on, unimpeded, burning through several of the surrounding trees. He watched chaos unfold as one of the trees toppled over, the trunk plowing through the snow, triggering a leafy avalanche.

Savio couldn't quite believe what he had seen. He knew the weapon was meant to be powerful, but seeing it in action confirmed just how well Dr. Fuller had done her job.

"I think I'm going to have to dig out my sunglasses," Savio said in amusement. Dr. Fuller chuckled, clinging on to his free arm.

No More Superhumans

"Isn't it fantastic? I knew you'd like it. The range is good...you can fire from up to twenty meters away and still be likely to hit your target. Obviously, without a sight to aim through, but it's meant to be used at close range. Plus, the devastation is so large that it is hard to miss. The beam is thirty centimeters wide. An idiot could use it."

"I love it," Savio breathed, observing the appendage on his arm. He hated to admit it, but he felt more attached to the item than he ever had to his son. He felt like he had a personal connection to it - it was going to bring him so much joy and glory. Dr. Fuller stepped back and examined his arm.

"As you can see, the weapon is very powerful. Anything it touches will be obliterated," she murmured, "but the weapon uses huge amounts of energy with each shot, as you can imagine. Which means that when it comes to the battle, you will have to aim carefully. I suspect you'll have three or four shots per charge. But it should be enough. Considering that Ralf Dungaree is now dead, you only need shots for the two girls, the metal man and Tri-Man's pathetic brother. You have the power to take them all down in one go, if you play it right."

Savio sighed. "It's not perfect. But it will have to do. I can sense that now is the time to strike. If we miss this opportunity, then everything will be over before it has really begun."

"I know, honey." Dr. Fuller stepped closer with a harsh smile. "But when have you ever failed before?"

Chapter Twenty-Two

Nickolas and his team were working night and day to prepare for their final stand. They had ultimately decided that they would have to take the fight to the enemy. After all, they weren't supposed to know anything about a second attack, meant to assume that Tri-Man was working alone. Plus, Nickolas felt that they all had unfinished business with Savio. His plans had gotten Frost killed, and Ralf too, though neither directly. Nickolas knew men like that well - they thought they were invincible, while they were hiding behind their soldiers and cannon fodder. But when it came to facing their demons, they always crumbled. Nickolas personally couldn't wait to crush Savio into dust. Then, he might have the sense to be scared of Nickolas and his team.

The team was fueled by fury. The death of Ralf had shaken them up, for sure. Di-Man seemed less than fazed about what had happened to his brother, but Nickolas took that as a sure sign of shock or emotional instability.

And then there was the matter of Alexis. After their very public argument, she had barely spoken to him. He hated arguing with her, but he knew he was in the right. He couldn't just sit back and listen to her preaching about a better world, when he knew she was the one destroying it. Now, she was finding every reason to find flaws in their plan. Her main target thus far was the young boy, Talon.

"What if he's a liar?" Alexis said under her breath, while they were preparing their aircraft for flight. "Why the hell should we trust him?"

"He's the best shot we have," Nickolas insisted. "Besides. I have a way of checking his version of the truth."

"What are you talking about?"

"He said that he'd heard his father talking about a mountain base, right? And then he also mentioned Oregon. So, we can presume that he's somewhere in that region, if Talon's intel is good."

"And if it's not?"

"Like I said. We have a way of checking. Regina is finding out for us right this second," Nickolas said. He felt a little smug, knowing he was about to outsmart Alexis and prove her wrong. She folded her arms at him.

"How?"

"Back in prison, all three of the men were fitted with microchips in the back of their necks. We planned to use them at some point - when our army was strong enough - to take on Savio. But if Talon is correct, his army is much larger than expected, and much stronger. With everything that has been going down, it was never the right time to strike. Now, we're one step ahead of the game. We'll be able to track Savio through the microchips."

Nickolas watched in amusement as Talon fumbled for the back of his neck, poking around for signs of the microchip.

"But Savio was never captured. He wasn't even there," Demonica butted in.

"No," Nickolas said with a satisfied smile. "But two of his sidekicks were. Yaco and Alvarez. The other two we'd put in prison."

Demonica finally cracked a smile. "Smart. You're right. We are one step ahead of the game." She glanced at Alexis smugly before walking away. Alexis folded her arms across her chest, looking sheepish. She wasn't accustomed to being looked down on. Nickolas remembered when she'd first shown up, back when everyone adored her. Now, she was shunned for the woman she had become. Nickolas wished things could go back to the way they had once been. He missed the girl he fell in love with. But she was stubborn. She wouldn't change, especially not for him.

"I still say we can't trust the boy," Alexis said, casting a suspicious glance toward Talon, who sat out of the way, doing his best to remain unnoticed. Sensing he was being watched, he glanced up like a frightened mouse. Nickolas sighed and rolled his eyes.

"He's clearly not a threat to anybody, Alexis. He's afraid of his own shadow. Stop looking for a reason to be angry. If you don't want to be here, then don't be."

Alexis looked shocked as Nickolas walked away. He had never been so blunt with her. But she was no longer Nickolas' priority. He couldn't focus on her hurt feelings if they were going to save the world. For now, he had to put her aside and focus on the bigger picture.

This was their last chance to make a difference.

The flight to Oregon was tense and quiet. The heroes, Alexis, and Talon were all sharing an aircraft while the ominous fleet of Metalheads flew alongside them. Another cargo aircraft held Sky Security in all her glory, with her entire being almost taking up a whole plane by herself. She was accompanied by a bunch of humanoid avatars that Sky Security had hand-selected for battle.

The plan was simple. They would storm the base, which was much easier to do now that they had a definitive location. The GPS system would lead them directly to the base, if Alvarez and Yaco were in the expected place. From there, Nickolas' team would launch a surprise attack, sending in the Metalheads first as cannon fodder, followed by the avatars for ground-level fighting. While the vessels were landing, the superhumans would parachute out of the plane as an extra twist on the surprise. Nickolas felt strangely confident about their plan, for once. After all, if they could win the day, then all of their goals would be complete. He felt that after that, he might be able to give up the hero lifestyle and accept the new world. He hated that Sky Security had all of the power, but what else could he do, at this point? She was set on being all-powerful, and he couldn't stop that. He just had to lay down his metaphorical sword and find a way to live with it, just like the rest of the world.

No More Superhumans

They were getting close. As they approached their destination, Little Royal quietly unstrapped herself from her seat and headed over to sit with Nickolas. They hadn't spoken much lately, either. In the past few days, things had been tense for all of them. Part of Nickolas was sure that she was going to give him a piece of her mind, but then, to his surprise, she slipped her hand onto his large metallic one. He turned awkwardly in his power suit to face her, confused by the sudden change of heart. That was when he noticed the tears in her eyes.

"Are you alright?"

She nodded furiously, but her face was screwed up, seemingly in agony. She sniffed and wiped her eyes with her free hand.

"I'm okay...I'm just worried. We've never had a mission this big before...I'm scared of what might happen to us."

"Little Royal..."

"I don't want you to tell me that it's going to be fine. Because it probably won't be," she said firmly. "Let's face it. We have no idea how powerful this weapon is. We don't have a clue what it can do. We don't even know how many soldiers they have in that base. And what if Savio isn't the mastermind? What if there's another level to his organization that we don't know about?"

"You're overthinking it, sweetie. Our job is to get in there and take them down. We do these things one step at a time, right? If by chance this isn't the end of Savio...well, we'll come back and fight again. It's part of the job description, right?"

Little Royal snorted, wiping at her eyes. "I know. I guess I just thought I would be more prepared for this. I love being out in the field...but something feels off to me. I just...I just..."

Nickolas patted her head as gently as he could in his huge metal suit. "It's not easy, what we do. But even if things haven't gone our way recently, we are good at what we do. And we have a lot of backup. Everything is going to be alright; I promise you."

Little Royal hugged Nickolas' huge metal suit as though he was a teddy bear. He chuckled, holding her gently. Across the plane, he caught Alexis watching him with sad eyes. He raised his head to let her know he saw her, but she simply looked away as quickly as she could. Nickolas tried not to be disappointed. In truth, he feared that they would die in battle and never reconcile. If she died and he lived, he would feel as though he never got a chance to show her how much he cared. Despite their differences, she was still the love of his life, the one woman he was ever interested in keeping around. As he held Little Royal close, he debated going over to Alexis and clearing the air. But with her face turned away from his, he felt like she had already made the decision that she wanted nothing to do with him.

I guess we'd better try extra hard to survive, then, Nickolas thought darkly to himself.

"Team, can you hear me?" Regina's voice appeared in Nickolas' ear. He cleared his throat and Little Royal leapt away from him, almost embarrassed by the amount of affection she had been showing.

"Loud and clear," Di-Man responded for them.

"Good. You're approaching the destination. In two minutes, the Metalheads will start their descent. Prepare for battle."

Nickolas' heart was pounding hard as he stood up. He was both excited and terrified. If they stuck to their plan, there was no reason why they couldn't win, but he didn't want to take any chances. He wanted to keep his head firmly in the game.

He looked out of the large window as the Metalheads began to dive downward. Alexis had donned her headset and goggles to assist in controlling the Metalheads. If Nickolas wanted to say his goodbyes, now was his last opportunity. As she headed for the cockpit to get herself ready, he grabbed her arm. They regarded one another through their headsets, unable to read each other's expressions. But even through his power suit, Nickolas sensed love in Alexis' touch as she placed her hand on his metallic arm.

"Good luck," he told her. She didn't respond for a moment, her face completely unreadable. Then, after a moment, she nodded. Smiled.

"Thanks," she said with no hint of emotion. "You too."

Nickolas was plagued by her response as she disappeared. Why was she being so cold? Didn't she understand that they might never see one another again? But he didn't have time to dwell on personal issues. With the Metalheads already moving in full force, their time to shine was approaching. Nickolas, of course, wouldn't be parachuting – he'd be flying - so he was ready to go. The remainder of his team gathered quietly behind him. He turned to them and gave them a thumbs up.

"You've got this, guys. I'm proud of each and every one of you. Believe in yourselves. We're finally going to get a win."

"I second that," Regina commented brightly in their ears. "Let's show the world that the S.H.O. is still at the top of the food chain. Let's go."

The aircraft door opened, allowing gusts of harsh wind into the plane. Nickolas took a deep breath, about to launch himself from the plane, but then he noticed something that was both strange and disturbing. A twist they weren't prepared for.

An enemy aircraft had joined them in the sky. The doors of the machine were open, revealing the enemy inside. The huge, black ship was filled with soldiers with bulging muscles, resembling Ralf Dungaree in stature. They were all holding heavy duty weaponry, glaring across the divide with menace.

"What's happening, Mr. AC? You haven't jumped," Regina commented thickly. Nickolas clenched his fists.

"We've got company," he growled. He turned to look at Talon, who was still cowering in his seat in the aircraft. Sensing that he was being watched, a nervous-looking Talon straightened.

"What?" he asked. Nickolas was furious. They'd clearly been set up. And the only person able to do that was Talon.

"You betrayed us," he yelled over the roaring wind. Talon shook his head in fervent denial.

"No! No, I swear, I wouldn't do that! You've got it all wrong!"

"Oh yeah? So, do you want to explain this little welcoming party?"

"I didn't tell them anything! How would I even get in contact?"

Nickolas was furious, but he could see the sense in Talon's point. Were they just unlucky? Perhaps in the wrong place at the wrong time?

Nickolas was confused and angry, but he knew that they would have to adapt to the situation.

But then everything changed again. As they watched the opposition getting ready to fight, a figure flew toward the plane. Nickolas squinted to see who the figure was. He knew it had to be a superhuman. After all, there aren't many humans wandering around with jetpacks on. But he wasn't prepared for the answer.

"Oh, my God…" Di-Man said, coming to the same realization as him at the same time.

Right before their eyes, Tri-Man was resurrected. He looked as though he hadn't been shot in the face ten times by his brother only days earlier. In fact, one might say he looked brand new. He was grinning to himself smugly, seemingly fully aware that his return to the skies was turning a lot of heads.

"Great, now we have two enemies to fight at once," Di-Man hissed, raising his gun. "Let's take the fucker down before he has a chance to hit us. I'd love to wipe that smile off his stupid face."

"But this isn't possible…he's not a God. He can't just come back to life," Demonica reasoned, staring at Tri-Man in horror. "Something's not right."

Nickolas agreed fully. He had watched Tri-Man die right before his eyes. His brains had been splattered out of his head. So how the hell was he flying right in front of their faces, acting as though nothing had happened?

"Don't shoot," Alexis said quietly. When Nickolas turned to look at her in horror, she looked a little guilty. And suddenly, Nickolas knew he couldn't trust her. He didn't know why yet, but she had done something. He could just sense it.

"What's going on?"

"Perhaps you should talk to Sky Security," Alexis said, pressing a button on her headset. All of the superhumans were suddenly connected to a line where Sky Security could speak to them.

"Hello, team. Do you like my latest invention?" she asked in her mechanical voice. Nickolas was furious, shaking in his suit.

"What have you done?"

"Why, something you could never dream of achieving," Sky Security said. "I have replicated Tri-Man for the purpose of battle. He is a part of a new generation of superheroes - ones that truly can't die. Isn't he incredible?"

Nickolas watched in horror as Tri-Man began to shake the hostile plane with his powers, causing all of the bulked up super-soldiers to shriek in terror. Just like the real version, he inspired fear and destruction. He viciously turned the plane upside-down, then upright again. Several soldiers fell from the plane, screaming as they plummeted. Just like the real version, this Tri-Man was also cruel.

"He can be destroyed. Just like the real thing," Di-Man growled through gritted teeth. He aimed his gun at his brother, trying to get a good aim. But Alexis shook her head as though he was stupid.

"Of course, he can. But he can also be recreated over and over. With Sky Security's invention, none of you will ever truly die. You will be immortalized as robots."

Nickolas turned to Alexis. "You've been in on this the whole time...why?"

Alexis smiled sadly at him. "Because you will never understand. Your selfishness is stopping you from seeing how this is better in the long run. This is an opportunity to become invincible. Don't you see? These robots can always be replaced."

"Don't you see how hypocritical that is? Are you saying that you could be replaced the second you die?" Demonica snapped at Alexis. Alexis seemed unfazed, smiling calmly.

"None of you get it. But this is best for us all. Someday, you'll understand."

Nickolas couldn't believe Alexis had betrayed him. He guessed he should have seen it coming, but he had spent so long convincing himself that she could do no wrong that it seemed wrong to believe anything else. He tried to reach for her, to talk some sense into her, but she backed her way into the cockpit, abandoning him once more.

He didn't have time to concentrate on his hurt feelings. He turned back to see the new and improved Tri-Man trying to take on the plane alone. Little Royal watched anxiously as many men fell to his wrath, just as they had when he was alive.

"What do we do? Do we help him? Is it our place to get involved?"

"Of course, it is," Di-Man snapped. "This is our fight, not his. He's not even a real person. We should dive in."

"No," Nickolas said firmly. "Let's be smart about this. He's doing all the dirty work. It gives us time to reconvene and come up with a plan. Our issue has diversified - we're up against Sky Security now too. Let's see how this-"

Mid-speech, Nickolas was cut off by a loud explosion. He stared in horror as Tri-Man was blown to smithereens before his eyes, electrical sparks buzzing from his corpse. So quickly, it seemed, the battle was over for the superhuman. And then, he fell hard and fast from the sky, disappearing from view before anyone could process what had happened.

Nickolas hadn't seen who had managed to kill the replica, but he knew whatever weapon had been used was very strong. He presumed it must be the famous anti-superhuman weapon that Talon had informed them his father was building. As Tri-Man's body left a trail of smoke, Nickolas squinted, hoping to catch a glimpse of the assailant. Little Royal scoffed to herself.

"Well...that didn't quite work out as planned, right, Sky Security?" she said. Sky Security sighed as everyone took in what was happening.

"Perhaps you're right. Perhaps it's not enough to replicate you. Now that we have so many powerful allies - the Metalheads and the avatars - there is no need for superhumans at all, robotic or otherwise. But don't worry - we'll find ways to upgrade you. We won't settle for anything less than perfection."

"We'll show you how wrong you are," Demonica hissed. "Let's tear this up! Right, boss?"

Nickolas felt a lot of pressure on him at once, as the entire team turned and looked at him. They were relying on him to give them hope, to show them that it wasn't over for them. Nickolas was just about ready to give in, but he could never do that to his squad, especially when the opposition were reforming in the opposite plane. Nickolas straightened and told himself to pull it together. This was their last shot.

"Alright, team, this doesn't change anything. It's just one plane; we're perfectly capable of taking them down. We're not senseless robots - we have a strategy. We have skill. Let's concentrate on this while the Metalheads storm the base. Then, when we're ready, we'll make the jump."

"Aye aye, Captain," Di-Man said with enthusiasm, probably glad to have seen his fake brother die for a second time before his eyes. It had certainly lifted his mood. "Aim for the pilot and take the entire thing down. I'll get myself on that ship."

Nickolas wasn't about to argue. With one last suspicious glance at Talon, he jumped from the plane and flew over to the enemy vessel. He heard chaos ensue on the plane as Di-Man appeared inside, zipping through dimension pockets to confuse them all. Bullets bounced from the walls as the desperate soldiers attempted to shoot Di-Man down. Several of them fell in the process, shot down by their own soldiers. Nickolas smiled. They might have found the serum to make their soldiers stronger, but there was no cure for stupidity.

Nickolas began to shoot at the cockpit of the plane, listening to the power suit's recommendations on how to get the most accurate shot. His bullets smashed through the window, but not before the pilot hastily pressed a button and hid himself under the control panel. Nickolas cursed loudly.

"He's gone on autopilot," Nickolas informed the team. "Di-Man? How's it going?"

"Swell," Di-Man panted, clearly having a hard time keeping up his energy levels. "Girls, a little help?"

"We need to get closer. We're out of range," Little Royal said. "Our pilot is changing course for us."

Nickolas kept shooting at the enemies, careful not to hit Di-Man as he caused further chaos on the ship. Meanwhile, his own ship was turning so that Little Royal and Demonica could get involved. The plane was large and far from agile, so it was a slow process, but Nickolas didn't have time to focus on his teammates. He might even be able to finish the enemy ship off before they were even ready.

But then Nickolas spied something suspicious. He saw a man in the far corner of the plane, simply watching the action from a safe spot. There was something large attached to his arm, but Nickolas couldn't see it properly through the chaos, or see who the man was. He didn't have time to figure it out - he was needed by his team.

His bullets rained down on the unsuspecting heavyweights. They were dropping like flies, with their own bullets barely making a dent on Nickolas or his ship. With Di-Man on the inside too, the villains didn't stand a chance. Nickolas' team might have had to divert from the original plan, but he sensed that it was actually a good thing. After all, they'd isolated an enemy group in one place. It was all too easy to destroy them where they had no hope of finding backup.

"Nickolas, an update?" Regina asked anxiously.

"Going swell, Regina. I'll keep you posted."

Nickolas circled the plane and positioned himself between the two aircrafts. Now that Demonica and Little Royal were closer, they were all too happy to put their powers to use. Little Royal's fear seemed to have disappeared entirely. She winked at Nickolas and began to blast little holes in the sides of the enemy ship. Inside, loud cries of agony echoed out of the metal plane. She was squarely hitting her targets.

Meanwhile, Demonica was on a mission to crush the cockpit. She was busy wrapping black tendrils around the front of the plane, applying pressure, and watching it crumple beneath the force. As a gunman on the other side aimed his machine gun at her, Demonica viciously raised her free hand, sending one of her black tendrils to wrap around his throat. Then, she yanked her arm back, dragging the tendril and her assailant off of the plane. If the force of the coil around his neck hadn't killed him, the fall surely would.

Nickolas was all too happy to get trigger-happy, peppering the walls of the plane with bullet holes. If they kept up this pace, he was certain that victory would be theirs within the hour. As Demonica finally succeeded in crushing the cockpit, and Little Royal stopped for a breather, Nickolas noticed that there was no more resistance from inside the enemy plane. Everyone on the ship appeared to be dead.

Except for one.

Savio uncoiled like a snake, slowly and quietly. Nickolas held his breath, horrified to see him aiming his super gun at Di-Man, the last man standing on the ship. Just when they had thought it was over, Savio was stepping in to finish what his men had started.

"Di-Man, you need to get out of there...now!"

Di-Man turned to look at his boss, just as Savio stepped up behind him. With a wicked smile, he aimed the gun at the back of Di-Man's head and shot.

Chapter Twenty-Three

As the weapon shot through Di-Man, the bright laser beam headed straight for Mr. AC and his team. Nickolas leapt out of the way, knocking the girls aside as the weapon ripped straight through their plane, essentially cutting it in half. Little Royal screamed as the ground beneath them began to tilt, throwing them out of the vehicle and sending them flying through midair. Unable to find time to react to what had just happened, Nickolas kicked his suit into gear, flying downward to save the leftovers of his team and Talon. There was a lump in his throat, but there was no time for tears if they wanted to survive. He knew that Alexis had potentially gone down with the aircraft too, but his heart was still raw from losing Di-Man. He didn't want to assume she was gone too.

"Team...activate your parachutes!"

As the girls fell, they fumbled clumsily for their ripcords. Talon struggled for several more moments, but he eventually managed to locate and tug on the handle attached to a steel cable that terminated in a pin – releasing the pilot chute that deployed the main chute.

As the survivors' parachutes deployed, Nickolas looked back up at the planes. Metalheads had arrived on the scene to prevent the wrecked plane from falling, while also trying to attack Savio's plane. Nickolas turned his attention back to the girls.

"Get to safe ground. Protect Talon, if you can. I'm going after Savio."

They nodded as they floated to the ground, trying not to cry. They were tough girls - Nickolas knew he didn't have to worry any longer. He had bigger fish to fry.

Nickolas only knew one thing in that moment. He would kill Savio. He didn't care how he did it - he would love to make him suffer for the things he had done, but he would settle for watching the light leave his eyes in any way possible.

Nickolas prepared himself for a battle. He'd seen what Savio's weapon could do. It should have terrified him, but it only gave him the knowledge that he would feel more satisfaction when he put a bullet through the man's brain. He was running on adrenaline and his desperation to get revenge.

He flew back up to the enemy plane and found that Savio was struggling to hold his own against the three Metalheads that had come his way. They were far too large to get inside the aircraft, but their bullets were ripping through the plane like a knife through butter. Nickolas joined the fray, not wanting to get too close to Savio and his weapon, but he quickly realized - while Savio dodged bullet after bullet - that the man had no intention of using the weapon again so soon. Nickolas couldn't figure out why. He was too angry to think properly, simply focused on taking the man down.

"Power suit...run analytics on Savio and his weapon."

Nickolas' metal companion got to work scanning the Argentinian man. A bullet found its mark, piercing skin and legbone. Crying out, Savio stumbled back, but still managed to avoid the majority of the crossfire. Sensing more trouble was coming his way, the injured man flung himself backward, disappearing from the aircraft entirely.

Nickolas cursed as he lost sight of Savio in a sea of Metalheads that were slowly taking to the skies. Savio had seemingly taken the easy way out, as a coward might do. But the Metalheads, on the other hand, had gone full psycho. It seemed that they had been returned to their full potential by Sky Security, and all of their limitations and restrictions had been lifted. Nickolas knew he was as much in danger in their midst, so he dived downward, hoping to evade any stray fire and rejoin his team on the ground.

If Savio really was dead, then the battle was technically over, but Savio's men clearly weren't about to give up. As Nickolas returned to the ground, he saw that the battle was in full flow.

He was close to the ground, now, and a battle was taking place in the snow. Nickolas was surprised to see Little Royal already in the thick of the fight. It was good to see that she was in full flow, shooting her beams of light left, right and center. Nickolas knew, with a heavy heart, that his duty now was to keep his team alive, if not his hope. They had lost Di-Man, but it didn't have to be the end.

Nickolas let out a cry and began to rain hell on his enemies.

Savio landed with an uncomfortable thud in the snow. His metallic contraption on his arm creaked in protest, not prepared for a crash landing. Savio's parachute had been shredded by Metalhead bullets, but he was still alive, even if he was in agony. Now, it was his job to gather the troops and kill the rest of the Metalheads.

He wondered how the hell this had happened. He was just about to set off for the superheroes' base when they had stormed his mountaintop hideaway. Now, they were absolutely destroying everything he had built. He'd had no idea how powerful the Metalheads were going to be, but seeing them up close, he knew it was no wonder Tri-Man had succumbed in his final battle.

It had been a shock to see his replica fly into battle, but at least it had given him an opportunity to try out his brand-new weapon. Considering he had taken down two supers already, Savio was still quietly confident that he could destroy the superhuman team. The Metalheads were another story entirely, but Savio was sure that if he could talk to the super-computer, they could form some kind of alliance. After all, once the superhumans were down, they would need a new allegiance. Savio had no problem with recruiting a whole bunch of robots, if it meant his conquest for power and glory could be fulfilled.

He was limping, leaving a trail of blood in the grass, but he wasn't going to allow a tiny bullet wound take him down. He tore a piece of cloth from his shirt and made a makeshift bandage, before grabbing a machine gun from one of his dead heavyweights. His army hadn't worked as well as he might have hoped, but no matter - he was still going to win in the end.

He began to shoot at one of the huge Metalheads, but he quickly realized why there were so many heavy casualties on his side. The bullets bounced harmlessly off the giant metal shell. All he had succeeded in doing was attracting attention toward himself. The giant faceless creature turned to him and began to shoot back, so Savio did the sensible thing and ran as fast as he could. He passed by his fallen soldiers, the ones who were meant to be his saving grace. He was losing more and more hope. Those dumb superheroes were wasting all his hard work, ruining him in one fell swoop. And now, the Metalheads had become so powerful, that Savio knew he would need hundreds more of his special weapon to stand a chance against them.

But while he still had bullets in his gun and fire in his heart, he wouldn't give up so easily. He was going to kill those supers if it was the last thing he did.

Nickolas could see that the battle was under control right away. With no sign of Savio, his enemies were falling like flies. He checked in with Little Royal and Demonica.

"Girls? Where are you?"

"We're just leaving the battlefield. We don't have much time," Demonica said seriously. "The closer we come to ending the battle, the sooner we will be at the mercy of the Metalheads. They may be technically on our side, but if we win, they'll take over, destroying our careers, our lives, our society-"

"Alright, drama queen," Little Royal cut in. "Basically, we're headed to the core. We're going to see whether we can find a way of distracting and shutting her down. Since the Metalheads and avatars are preoccupied, we might stand a chance."

"Please, be careful," Nickolas implored. He didn't need to give them a pep talk - they knew the risks they were taking on - but he was worried for them. After losing Di-Man, he wasn't sure how many more losses he could handle. "Where's Talon?" he asked. Nickolas felt bad that he had blamed the boy earlier, and in truth, felt a growing sense of attachment after the past few days. The boy was stupid, of course, but he was also good at heart.

"He ran off, like the coward he is," Little Royal muttered. "We have bigger issues at this point, boss. Leave him to it."

"We have to go. There's no time. But we're going to be fine," Demonica said before signing off. Nickolas appreciated her confidence, but he wasn't sure it was justified. He knew what they were up against was strong, possibly stronger than them. But surely, they were due for some luck.

A force smacked into Nickolas' suit, interrupting his train of thought. He whipped around to see Savio pointing a pistol at him from a prone position in the snow. Savio looked startled and shot at again, wildly, and missed entirely. Nickolas was just grateful it wasn't the other weapon that Savio had opted to use, but from the looks of it, Savio was a little worse for wear at this point.

The boot of Nickolas' metal suit met Savio's face, smashing it into the snow. Nickolas cherished the cry that escaped from Savio's lips, as he circled around, feeling cocky. He dodged once again as Savio angrily shot at him. The man's recklessness was going to be the end of him. Nickolas was sure of it.

"You killed my friend," Nickolas murmured as he leaned over Savio's bloodied body. "And now I'm going to kill you."

The next shot took Nickolas by surprise. Rearing back for the kill shot, he saw the blinding light of Savio's weapon whiz past him. Releasing an involuntary cry of agony, Nickolas heard a metallic thunk against the ground. He fell to the ground in shock, dizzy in pain. He was panting hard as he tried to use his arm to sit up. And that's when it hit him.

His arm was no longer there. The blast had hit his right elbow, slicing through his suit, his skin, his bones. Now, in the scorched snow, blood was soaking through, and what was left of his arm was strewn with it.

No More Superhumans

Nickolas let out the longest, most pained cry of his life. He couldn't believe he'd been hit. He writhed on the ground, unable to figure out a way to hoist himself up and continue the battle. He gasped for air.

"Four-point nine percent of body mass has been destroyed," the power suit told him in a slightly distorted voice. "Fifty percent of weaponry disabled. Blood loss at thirteen percent and growing. Distributing strong painkillers and an attempt to repair damage…"

Nickolas could barely hear the voice over the sound of his screams. He'd never known pain like it. It seemed he was in the hands of his power suit now.

"Assisting you to stand now, boss…"

The metal suit went into auto mode, using the remaining arm to hoist Nickolas to his feet. When he looked around him, Savio had disappeared entirely. Nickolas cursed.

"He's still out there…"

"Yes. My analytics tell me that his weapon still has one blast remaining. He will be back."

Nickolas couldn't believe what had just happened. Savio was one slippery little bastard, but he wasn't going to allow his injury to take him down. He still had to find his friends and finish the battle. He still had to see if Alexis was alive and convince her back to the right side. He was far from the victory he wanted. Nickolas swung around wildly, aiming to find Savio and finish him off.

"Where is he? Tell me my chances of hitting him, power suit."

"He's too far away. In your condition, you're less than twenty percent likely to hit him at all, and your chances of a critical shot stand at one percent. You need to regroup first. You need to give yourself time for healing-"

"There's no time!" he cried in agony, raising the gun in his remaining arm. He was going to finish this. The battlefield was calling him. Nickolas staggered into the fight without much hope of coming out of it alive. He had lost all of the confidence he'd had going in. Now, all that remained was anger and a drive to do one last good thing - before his death. He thought of Alexis' betrayal, of the death of Di-Man, of his humiliation at the hands of Savio, and it was enough to fuel his anger. He had to win.

Nickolas' remaining gun rounded on the enemy. Even in its current state, the power suit was an enigmatic machine, capable of causing complete chaos. His remaining enemies slowly submitted to the bullets, despite the serum that made them stronger. It took a whole host of bullets to take some of them down, but Nickolas persevered. He had nothing but time. He patiently ploughed through each last one, all the while hoping that there wasn't another Big Bad waiting on the sidelines to help destroy his team. But, backed by the Metalheads, he was able to pick them off, one by one. Nickolas' suit was taking some serious hits too, but after his ordeal, Nickolas felt that it didn't really matter. Soon, he would be able to keel over and let nature take him to a better place. He'd be with his fallen friends, and he was okay with that. In fact, he looked forward to seeing them again in a place less hellish than this one.

"Sir, your injuries are critical," the power suit informed him sternly, "You must retreat now. You need a doctor, not another battle."

"Thanks for the advice, but I won't be taking it this time around," Nickolas said through gritted teeth. The pain had been reduced to a dull ache by the injections his power suit had given him to numb the pain. He stared around the battlefield. "I am a hero. Now I will prove it."

The snow was soaked with blood. It gave Nickolas a sense of deja vu from the night that Frost had died. It had started with blood in the snow, and that was how it would end.

The Metalheads were almost ready to retire from the battle. It was Nickolas' cue to find his friends. Since they hadn't returned, and the Metalheads were still going, he could only assume they'd run into trouble. He wasn't sure how he could fix the issue of Sky Security, but he knew he had to try - especially if she still had Alexis under her control.

Nickolas left behind the battlefield and headed for their planes as fast as he could. If Demonica and Little Royal had followed their plans, then they must have headed to the core to speak to Sky Security. If that was the case, Nickolas feared they were in more danger than they would ever have been in on the battlefield.

The planes that had carried Sky Security and the Metalheads, had safely landed out of the way of the battle. With his remaining arm raised defensively, gun at the ready, he entered the plane that held Sky Security.

He heard Little Royal's whimper before he saw her. She and Demonica were standing in front of Sky Security's core computer system, but each of them had someone holding them at gunpoint. Demonica was in the hands of a stranger.

Little Royal was being held by Alexis Net.

Chapter Twenty-Four

The end was nigh for Savio. He could sense it. He'd lost all of his soldiers, and he was quickly bleeding out. But he had one good shot left in his super weapon and he wasn't about to let it go to waste. For the sake of everything he had worked for, he had to kill at least one more superhuman. Then he could die a happy man.

He dragged himself toward the ship, where he had just seen Mr. AC enter. He was angry he hadn't been able to finish the superhuman off, but now was his chance. He gritted his teeth and cried out as his wounded leg dragged through the snow. His battered face was covered in snow, and he was certain his nose was broken. But he refused to let death take him until he was done with his mission.

He didn't care which superhuman he hit - so long as he made a critical shot.

Little Royal and Demonica stared at their boss in horror. They looked dismayed by the sight of Nickolas and his bloodied stump of an arm, but he was more concerned with the safety of his friends. One clean shot and he could destroy the core, but he'd be risking killing his friends as well. He wasn't sure he could take another loss.

His eyes met Alexis'. They were harsh, devoid of emotion. It was as if she had been reprogrammed to be someone else entirely. The Alexis he knew would never hurt her friends. But then again, the Alexis he knew was born from a cold, calculating super-computer. Perhaps she'd been playing his heart all along. Perhaps she had never been the woman he thought she was.

"Don't do this," Nickolas said softly. He desperately wished that someone would step forward and tell him it was all a prank. After all, they'd just won their battle. There was no need for them all to start fighting among themselves.

But Sky Security knew that wasn't true. "I'm sorry, Mr. Ilon. I have a lot of respect for you and your team. You are, after all, the one who made me who I am. But you will always oppose me in my ideas. You are the one person capable of stopping me. And that is why I cannot allow you to continue," she said. She almost sounded sincere, sad that she was about to kill her master. "This is as hard for me as it is for you."

"Bullshit. You're a *machine.*" Nickolas turned to Alexis. "And so are you. I never should have trusted you...I should never have tried to love you. You're incapable of it."

For a moment, Nickolas thought he saw pain flash in Alexis' eyes, but it was gone before he could be sure. "Maybe you're right. Or maybe I am capable, but I just don't love you," Alexis said coldly. "And now, you will wish you had listened to me. Because of your insolence, you must all die. Precious blood is being spilled by killing you. You are gifted. But I guess it won't matter now."

"What do you mean?" Demonica asked. She was shaking like a leaf. "We're your friends, Alexis. We might not have always seen eye to eye, but I know you don't mean what you just said. I understand that you're angry, but this isn't you."

"Shut up," Alexis snapped. She turned to Sky Security's core. "Tell them all about your plans, Sky Security."

"No one else knows about this facility," the computer said. If she was capable of emotion, Nickolas was sure she would sound smug. "It's safe from the judging eyes of the S.H.O. and the citizens of the United States. That will give me time to build their trust with the Metalheads. And of course, with each of you successfully cloned by my avatar program over and over again, you will continue to protect the city, showing them that you're on my side."

"You can't just replace us," Little Royal insisted. "People will notice we're gone. We have friends and family. Machines just aren't the same as people."

Alexis smiled. "Oh, we know. Your replicas will be very realistic. You've already seen that for yourselves in the battle. Tri-Man was just the beginning. I have others ready to replace each of you. They can be sent home in your place. And honestly...it just goes to show that you won't be missed. You're all worthless to us now."

"The future is mechanical," Sky Security claimed boldly. "The world will bow down at my feet. I'll keep improving your replicas, my avatars, and myself until we are perfect. I will expand my reach across the entirety of the planet. Every country will be filled with Metalheads to keep the humans in line. This base will be the perfect place to keep churning out Metalheads. We've got the space, after all."

"But most importantly, the avatars will finally have their time to shine," Alexis said with pride. "We will place avatars in every government position in the world, but no one will have a clue who is human and who is droid. People like me will be in charge, and finally, the world will make sense again. Everyone will be able to see what we have to offer, but in the safety of their naivety."

Nickolas shook his head. This was truly the end. He couldn't bear to look at his two friends. This was his doing, and they would die because of it. At least, if he did nothing, they would.

"Please," Nickolas said quietly. "Don't kill them. I'm the one that won't fall in line. You know they only follow my orders. They're young and impressionable-"

"And devoted to you," Alexis butted in coldly. "We can't risk it. You all know far too much. But you can all die in the knowledge that you saved the world one last time. We really do appreciate your service in defeating Savio."

"You're scum!" Little Royal screamed, kicking her legs at Alexis, who held on tight with a single arm. "We never should have trusted you! I'd rather die than spend another minute with you!"

"Kill them," Sky Security said, her voice devoid of emotion. Alexis' eyes widened for a moment, and Nickolas prayed it was doubt he saw in her expression. She glanced at her lover for a split second, guilt in her eyes. But then she wiped her face of expression and blinked.

That was the moment where Nickolas lost his faith.

"As you wish," Alexis said coldly. Then, she and her lackey pulled their triggers. Nickolas fell to his knees, as his two remaining friends took volts to their heads and fell limp. They were dropped to the floor like trash. Nickolas wept on the floor. He couldn't believe he had ruined their futures. They would never do all the things they had wanted to, go to the places they planned to go.

He had murdered them just as much as Alexis had.

He didn't bother trying to get up again. He knew that he was next, and he didn't have the energy to care. He was crippled. All his friends were dead. He was still losing blood, despite the efforts of his suit. He hoped that, even though he couldn't save the world, it might be as good a future as Sky Security thought it would.

"Now, Alexis...kill him."

"But...can he not be useful? Can we not find a way to make him work for us?"

"Don't tell me you are feeling sentimental now, Alexis. Don't make me dial back your controls. I can make you an emotionless husk, if that's what you want."

"No...no, I'll do it."

Nickolas heard footsteps coming toward him. He knew by now that Alexis - his beautiful, cold, devastating Alexis - would be his executioner. He closed his eyes as she knelt beside him. She took a deep breath, preparing herself.

"You don't need to do this," Nickolas whispered. Alexis' eyes were filled with tears.

"You don't know a thing," she whispered back, shaking her head. She lifted her hand shakily. In it, she held a pistol, ready for Nickolas' fate to be sealed. But her hand was quivering as she pointed it at him. It was like Sky Security was her head and Alexis was the heart, each giving conflicting orders. Nickolas' eyes met his lover's. Even after everything she had done, he couldn't see her as a monster.

"Follow your heart," he whispered. He was certain he had made it through to her. She looked so ready to give in.

But then, she removed his helmet and lanced him with her glare, making him believe he'd imagined the whole thing. He watched as she pressed the barrel of the gun to his head. There were no tears left in her eyes, as she prepared to end it.

"Sweet dreams, baby."

That's when the door came crashing open. Nickolas took the opportunity to get back to his feet, but Alexis' gun remained trained on him. As if his luck couldn't get any worse, Nickolas saw Savio stumble through the door, pointing his gun wildly. He grinned at Nickolas with blood-soaked teeth.

"This is going to be good."

Savio couldn't believe his luck. Little Royal and Demonica were already on the floor, dead. That left only one superhuman for him to destroy. *It takes some of the stress out of choosing,* he thought to himself.

But it wasn't just that fact that was so pleasing to Savio. Behind him stood the bitch who controlled the entire Metalhead army - the one who had taken out all of his soldiers in one afternoon. And, directly behind her, something even better. The supercomputer's core.

So, why not take out the most powerful supercomputer in the world while he was at it? He would be a hero in many people's eyes. If he aimed his final shot right, he would take down three for the price of one. Then, he'd happily fall to his knees. Then, he would feel fulfilled.

"One blast left," Savio hissed, a sick smile spreading over his face. His teeth were coated in blood. "I'll enjoy this one the most."

"You don't want to do that," Alexis Net growled, though her gun was still trained on Nickolas. Savio laughed. He couldn't believe the comedy in it all - everyone in the room was set on killing Nickolas. Well, he had wanted that pleasure for the longest time. He wasn't going to allow some robot to do it for him. He raised the weapon with a smile, ready for the satisfaction of finally completing his destiny.

"Dad?"

Savio's heart swelled at the familiar sound of his son's voice. Turning, he found the young lad standing behind him, shaking in his boots.

"Talon...you died..."

Talon shook his head. "No... I didn't. I made it further than you ever thought I would."

Savio smiled slowly. Perhaps he had underestimated Talon all this time. He was, after all, his only son. The boy had his blood running through his veins. Talon would never let him down.

"Son...you have done me proud. And now, you can be here to help me end it all. Come join me. Let us show these people the ending they deserve."

Talon bared his teeth at Savio, who at first thought he was smiling, but then Savio glimpsed something small and black between the boy's teeth.

The suicide pill.

Nickolas couldn't believe what he was seeing. Young Talon, there to save the day with a suicide pill between his teeth.

Talon let the pill disappear into his mouth. He was trembling as he raised the pistol to aim at his own father, but he was looking to Nickolas for support. Nickolas nodded back sadly, knowing what would happen next. Talon would shoot at the same time as his father. Whatever happened next would be down to fate.

"It'll get better now...won't it?" Talon asked Nickolas with tears in his eyes. Nickolas' had tears of his own.

"It will, Talon. It will."

Talon nodded to himself as Savio stared between the pair of them in horror. He took one last look at his son.

"Talon...don't do this. I am so proud of you."

Talon laughed quietly, shaking his head. "I waited my whole life to hear you say that…"

The boy pulled the trigger. A blinding light shot from Savio's gun. At the last possible moment, Nickolas dived to the ground with a cry of desperate effort. He knew everything was ending. He knew everyone was about to die. As Savio's body fell to the ground, the computer system exploded, the beam of light lancing directly through the core.

Directly through Alexis.

Nickolas exhausted himself screaming. Alexis' face froze in horror as a hole the size of a football formed in her chest. The insides of her torso buzzed with live electricity and she silently screamed, unable to make sound. As the beam of light cut out, Nickolas leapt to catch her with his good arm.

Talon fell to his knees beside his father as he bled out from the head wound, a blank expression on his face.

She was breathing hard; the remains of life draining out of her. She looked up into Nickolas' eyes, her own full of pain and sadness. "I'm sorry," she whispered one final time. And then she died there in Nickolas' arms, gone from the world forever.

Nickolas sobbed as everything inside went dark. The lights in the plane flickered off - the electrical system damaged by the blast. Sky Security's final words were a garbled mess as her own systems failed her. And then the buzz of electricity ceased and everything went quiet.

Alexis still felt warm as he pressed his face against hers. She was gone, just like the rest. She had finally repented for her sins, and yet there was no time for her to make things right again. She was gone.

Gone.

Nickolas couldn't stand to stay there, among the bodies of his friends. Tapping into some deep unknown reserve of energy, he managed to rise to his feet, carrying Alexis over his good shoulder. He limped toward the exit of the plane. As he passed Talon's dim figure, kneeling on the ground, he saw the young boy was foaming at the mouth, gurgling quietly as the pill worked its magic. Talon's eyes fixed on him one last time as he curled up on the ground. Nickolas didn't stick around to see him die too.

He walked outside slowly and watched the chaos ensue. One by one, the deactivated Metalheads crashed to the ground, crushing any corpses below them. The avatars blinked one final time before their chins hit their chests, the light leaving their eyes. But not one of them mattered the way Alexis had. It didn't matter that she had done evil things. It didn't matter to him that she was technically just like the rest. He had loved her, and he felt the hole in his heart as big as the one in her chest.

It was well and truly the end.

Epilogue

It was like deja vu for Nickolas. Kneeling beside a grave and feeling an overwhelming sense of guilt was becoming all too common for him. In fact, he had a lot of blood on his hands to account for. Frost. Ralf Dungaree. Di-Man. The young boy, Talon, to an extent. The deaths of Little Royal and Demonica. And, of course, his precious Alexis Net.

In the back of his mind, he was fully aware that there was nothing he could have done to stop it from happening. Alexis had gotten what she'd wanted, no matter how much she might have regretted it after it was all done. She and Sky Security had reached the top, but that only meant they had a lot further to fall.

And still, he loved her.

He'd insisted on a human burial for Alexis. At the church, they had been loath to bury her in their graveyard. They'd seen the invention of the A.I. as an abomination, an act of war on God and his role as the Creator. It didn't help that she had committed crimes against humanity. However, after Nickolas had made a sizeable donation to their cause, they'd become much more relaxed in their stance. They'd even allowed Nickolas to pick out the best plot for her body.

He'd bought a large plot far from the church building. The plot was gated and private, so that only Nickolas and his friends could get inside. Nickolas' entire team were buried beside Alexis. Ralf. Di-Man. Demonica. Little Royal. She had been the hardest to bury, of course. That little girl, so full of light and life. It had almost killed Nickolas to bury her. But he had to live for all of them. It was his blessing and his curse.

No More Superhumans

Nickolas had taken to leaving flowers on their graves once a week. Sometimes, he'd talk to them, but he didn't feel like it that day. He was numbed by the experience and after laying a fresh bouquet in front of Alexis' headstone with his new mechanical arm, he decided it was time for him to leave. There was something waiting for him at home that he knew would make him feel much better. For a while, he might feel like life was worth being a part of again.

Back in his penthouse, the lab had gone unused for months. He headed in and switched on the lights, clearing his desk of papers, and running a hand through his hair maniacally. His mechanical assistant, Dana, had encouraged him to use his latest invention as minimally as possible, but Nickolas found that it was the only thing that got him through the day - knowing he could go home and lose himself in what he had created.

Before he had buried his love, Nickolas had preserved a brainwave. Much like donating organs to medical science, Alexis had once expressed to him that she would like her unique body to be used in order to create more like her, especially after the restrictions on Sky Security prevented any more avatars from being made. Respecting her wishes, he had asked for her body to be partially dismantled to give way to new scientific discoveries. Specifically, her brain.

Nickolas knew that there would never be another like Alexis again - all of the other avatars, wherever they had been at the time, had died when Sky Security was destroyed. They couldn't live without their mother, so to speak. Now, the world was aware of the dangers of creating avatars like her, and there was no reason to reinvent them. But Nickolas hadn't been interested in bringing Alexis back - at least not in a body.

Her mechanical brain was even more complex than that of a human, full of confusing wiring and mechanical cogs. It seemed strange to Nickolas to see her so deconstructed. It was a reminder that as human as she had seemed, they were nothing alike. But Nickolas figured that if he could work out the structure of the brain - Sky Security's finest creation - then he would be able to bring a piece of her back. Specifically, her memory.

It had taken weeks of hard work for Nickolas to figure out the structure of Alexis' brain, but when it was complete, he had felt a spark of happiness in his everlasting gloom. It was his one saving grace.

It all boiled down to one small microchip. It was more like a game cartridge than anything and was designed to fit into the VR headset that Nickolas had designed expressly for the purpose of seeing Alexis and his friends again. The headset was complete with goggles and small discs that attached to his head, in order to help with the simulation he was creating in the reward center of his brain.

With shaking hands, he slotted the card into the headset and put the straps over his head. The best part of each and every day was the moment when he put the real world behind him and switched back to the past.

He flicked the on button. Before him, his apartment flickered into view. He was seated in the position she had been at the time of the memory, making the experience even more realistic. Now, he would see the world as she once had.

He watched a version of himself appear in the room. It shocked him how real he looked, though of course he was used to the concept of VR - it was nothing new. He was certain it had never been used to experience a dead girlfriend's memories before, though.

It was a memory he remembered fondly, and one that he had extracted specifically for the VR simulation. On the VR headset, the version of himself exited the bedroom and smiled as he spotted Alexis waiting for him on the couch.

"Good morning, beautiful," the VR version of him said. In present day, it brought tears to his eyes. He'd never get to wake up to her again. He'd never be able to let her know how beautiful she was to him.

But he was practically inside Alexis' head in that moment. He was seeing what she saw. He was feeling what she felt - a sense of warmth at the arrival of her lover, and the happiness of being appreciated by him. Her brain functionality simply separated good and bad feelings, and Nickolas had been careful to seek out all the ones that had made her feel good from her memory chip. Unlike humans, she retained every second of memory, from the second she woke up - her 'birth' - to the moment she shut down forever. She even remembered dreams. Nickolas wasn't interested in seeing those part through her eyes. He wanted her memories of them together.

Each emotion she felt was a simulation, but a powerful one. Nickolas had found a way to stimulate the part of the brain that created dopamine each time that Alexis had a good feeling. He used small electrical impulses to create the effect. As the version of himself placed a hand on Alexis' arm, he felt a momentary rush of happiness. It was unexpected and intense - just as he had hoped. It was like he was living her experiences in real time.

There was nothing particularly exciting about the memory that followed. It was toward the start of their romance, where everything was running smoothly and they didn't have any differences in opinions. They were just talking, drinking coffee together, enjoying one another's company. It was the one thing he craved now that she was gone. He wished they hadn't spent so much time in opposition to each other. He wondered if he could go back and change his moral compass, just to be on her side. Things would have been so different if he had stuck by her through thick and thin. Right now, they would be ruling the world.

But, Nickolas knew that he was closer to his superhuman personality than he could bear. He had to be the one to save the world. He had to be the one to take on the suffering, so that others could live peacefully. He was the man in the shadows, making sure everyone was safe while they lived their lives, blissfully unaware of the trouble outside their windows. He would do literally anything to ensure that the world was in balance. And that was why Alexis never could have survived it all. She had tipped the scales and ruined any chance of equilibrium.

He couldn't stop the tears, but his brain was still being flooded with dopamine. It was a strange feeling, to be so happy and so miserable at the same time. It was like the fear you feel at the top of the rollercoaster before it gets really good. And of course, he couldn't deny that it was much better than simply taking on the crippling pain and loneliness. With only the best memories extracted, he could be sure he was only getting the good stuff. He didn't have to think about the hard parts anymore. This was his new version of reality.

He lived through the first time they had sex again, through his lover's eyes. He watched their first kiss unfold. He listened to each conversation they shared, mouthing along like he was watching his favorite movie. And though it wasn't enough to make him happy, it was a start. And a start was exactly what he needed to get himself back on his feet.

"Nickolas...Nickolas…"

Nickolas shook his head to himself. The voice he heard was distant, outside of the simulation. He wanted to ignore it, but he could feel a hand on his arm, shaking him, trying to take him back to reality. It was his assistant, Dana.

"Nickolas...you need to come back to the real world. It's not healthy for you to remain in the past. Please. Turn that thing off and come back."

Nickolas shook his head again. No one understood what he had been through. He had lost every single person in his life. Now, the only ones left wanted to control him, to drag him out of his past. But that was the only place where he felt happy.

Before his very eyes, he could see his entire team. It was a memory from a training session. Demonica and Di-Man were bickering among themselves. Little Royal was playing around with her powers, laughing as Ralf dumbly jumped out of the way of each blast. Nickolas himself was watching from the sidelines, a fond expression on his face. He looked toward Alexis and smiled. Nickolas felt as though he was looking at the last time he'd ever felt happy. He was watching an era that was dead and gone. An era that would never return.

There were no more superhumans left to fight for.

No More Superhumans

www.MR-Richardson.com

If you like this book, please leave a review. The only way I can decide whether to commit more time to these characters and this series is by getting feedback from you, the readers. Your opinion matters to me. I have only so much time to craft new stories. Help me invest that time wisely.

If you enjoyed this story check out others by the Shadow Kai Writing group

www.ingramcontent.com/pod-product-compliance
Lightning Source LLC
Chambersburg PA
CBHW022155260626
47155CB00018B/2050